Bold Beauty

✦✦✦✦✦

Winnie

The Horse Gentler

3

Tyndale House Publishers, Inc.
Carol Stream, Illinois

Bold Beauty

DANDI DALEY MACKALL

Visit the exciting Web site for kids at www.tyndale.com/kids and the Winnie the Horse Gentler Web site at www.winniethehorsegentler.com.

You can contact Dandi Daley Mackall through her Web site at www.dandibooks.com.

Tyndale Kids logo is a trademark of Tyndale House Publishers, Inc.

Bold Beauty

Designed by Jacqueline L. Nuñez

Edited by Ramona Cramer

Scripture quotations are taken from the *Holy Bible,* New Living Translation, copyright © 1996, 2004, 2007 by Tyndale House Foundation. Used by permission of Tyndale House Publishers, Inc., Carol Stream, Illinois 60188. All rights reserved.

For manufacturing information regarding this product, please call 1-800-323-9400.

ISBN 978-0-8423-5544-5, mass paper

Printed in the United States of America

15 14 13 12 11 10
12 11 10 9 8 7

*To Uncle Dick and
Aunt Mary Lou—
Thanks for your gentle,
helpful spirits.*

$\mathcal{W}$innie Willis, known the world over as "Winnie the Horse Gentler," breezes into the lead on her famous Arabian, the great Nickers. Three more jumps and the Grand National Championship title will be hers!

A hush falls over the crowd as horse and rider approach the fallen-log hurdle. They canter in straight. They're up and over! Now they circle left, the tall—okay, short—dark-haired girl flowing as one with her white mare. Nickers strides for the bush hurdle. Winnie is the only rider ever to jump bareback in this event. The powerful horse gathers strength in her haunches. No hesitation. They charge! They leap. . . . Yes! A clean jump, and the crowd goes wild!

"Winnie!"

Lizzy's voice reached the pasture, jerking me back to reality.

I brought Nickers down to a trot and stroked her neck under her flowing white mane. "Good girl. Almost had it, didn't we?"

I eyed the big hedge, the last jump in my imaginary steeplechase, the open-country horse race over nature's hurdles. I wouldn't have tried Nickers over the hedge anyway. My Arabian is the best horse in the universe, but she's not a hunter. Hunters are horses born to jump anything they come up against. The five-foot hedge would have been pushing it for Nickers. But I had to wonder what it would feel like.

"Winnie!" Lizzy called again, stepping back from the fence as I rode into the paddock and slid off Nickers. My sister collects lizards, admires bugs, and lately has developed a fondness for spiders. But she can't stand horses. It's her only fault.

"Richard Spidell called, Winnie. 'Winifred should have been here to clean stalls hours ago!' he said. I told him school had only been out an hour and his watch must be broken because you were really only 15 minutes late and would he like me to give him the name of a super watchmaker, meaning our dad, of course. Can Dad fix watches? So he said he didn't have time to talk with *little girls,* like I was one and he was the president or something. So I said—"

"Thanks, Lizzy." I had to stop her or I really would be hours late. Lizzy talks faster than a trotter trots. She's 11, a year younger than me, but taller and minus my freckles.

Lizzy still wore her school clothes, a fall green shirt that matched her eyes and my eyes, and twill pants like most kids in my middle school wore. I still wore my school clothes, but only because they were the same as my riding clothes—jeans and a T-shirt.

"It stinks that you have to shovel manure for the Spidells again! And on a perfectly good Friday afternoon." Lizzy handed me the soft-bristled brush and backed away again.

I shrugged.

The Spidells own every big business in Ashland, Ohio—Pizza-Mart, A-Mart Department Store, Pet-Mart, and Stable-Mart, their sorry excuse for a horse stable.

Back when we lived in Wyoming, my mom had a real ranch, where we gentled horses. But after Mom died, Dad sold the ranch. Then we moved eastward, zigzagging across the *I* states—Illinois, Indiana, and Iowa—and finally landing in Ashland, Ohio, where I hoped to spend my whole seventh-grade year. The first thing I'd done to help was get a job mucking stalls at Spidells' Stable-Mart.

Since then, though, I'd started my own horse gentling business, putting to good use everything Mom had taught me. And I'd quit my mucking job. But it was the first day of fall, and I hadn't had a new client since Labor Day. So, since most people put off horse training until spring, I'd gone back to mucking at Spidells'.

"It's not so bad, Lizzy." I brushed Nickers' white coat against the grain, then smoothed it back down. "Winnie the Horse Gentler is still in business. I just don't want Dad to have to pay for Nickers' upkeep all winter."

Towaco, my friend Hawk's Appaloosa, whin-nied from the field, wondering what was taking Nickers so long.

"I couldn't keep charging Hawk gentling fees for Towaco," I explained. "And the boarding fees won't carry us to spring."

Victoria Hawkins, a.k.a. "Hawk," had been my first client. Towaco had come along fast, settling down almost on his own once I got him out of Stable-Mart, the sterile horse factory where horses mean about as much as anchovy pizza at Pizza-Mart or plastic umbrellas at A-Mart.

I turned Nickers out into the pasture. She kicked up her heels and galloped to Towaco. She still took my breath away.

"Besides, I have a plan." I hadn't even totally formed it in my mind.

"A plan? Winnie? It's not going to get you in trouble, is it?"

"Down, Lizzy." She followed me toward the house. A flock of geese honked overhead. "I guess it's more like a mission." My secret mission explained why jumping had been on my mind all week, why I'd been practicing over low hurdles with Nickers. "Richard and Summer Spidell are working the most beautiful, deep chestnut hunter, Lizzy. Wait 'til you see her! It's like God created that horse to fly! But the Spidells are ruining her." I took a deep breath. "I have to help that beautiful mare before it's too late."

"Wi-n-n-ie?" Lizzy's voice sounded so much like our mom's when she'd known I was up to something that my breath stuck in my windpipe.

"Like Summer is just going to hand that horse over to you? I don't think so!"

Summer Spidell and I had gotten into it even before school started. And Richard, Summer's 16-year-old brother, considered himself my boss since I worked for his dad. They're what Mom called "horse possessors." Instead of loving horses, they possess them for profit or pride.

"Lizzy, you should see what they're doing to that mare!" A picture of Richard on the hunter flashed into my mind. I could see every outline of the mare's muscles, rippled like a bronzed statue of a war hero's steed.

When I was a little kid, I'd had my memory tested with 19 other guinea-pig kids. I was the only one who came out with the label "photographic memory." I remember being surprised—not that my mind could take pictures and store them in absolute detail, but that it didn't happen to everybody.

If I could have controlled the "camera" in my head, I'd have taken a shot of the hunter running free in the pasture. Instead my mental picture showed Richard smacking Bold Beauty for refusing the high jump.

I shook my head to empty out the image. "Lizzy, that horse came to Stable-Mart because she'd refused a couple of high jumps. She was edgy, but not scared of everything like she is now."

"Just be careful, Winnie. Don't get fired . . . again. Dad would freak."

Lizzy was right about the Dad freaking part. It hadn't been easy getting Dad to trust me with my horse business. Getting fired wouldn't exactly help my image. Besides, Dad and horses didn't mix. I'd never seen him ride. When we had the ranch, if Mom took a spill, she'd keep it from Dad so he wouldn't worry. Mom used to say she knew how much Dad loved her because he put up with her passion for horses.

I had to admit our dad was doing the best he could with two girls to raise on his own, especially since nobody ever claimed Winnie Willis was easy.

In Wyoming, I'd helped Mom with the horses, soaking up the way she got their trust and kept it. Dad used to travel into Laramie six days a week to boss people around in an insurance company. When Mom was killed in a car accident, Dad and I lost the only thing we had in common. It was taking time to get each other's trust and keep it.

"Don't worry, Lizzy. I'm just making friends with Bold Beauty in between her horrible practices with Richard."

"Bold Beauty? You named her already?"

Lizzy had never hung around with Mom and me when we gentled horses. But she knew our secret—that we tried not to name a horse we couldn't keep. It was hard enough giving them back to their owners. Still, since we needed to call them something, we'd make up names that described them. Mom would have liked the name Bold Beauty.

We reached the maple where Lizzy fed her lizards. She squatted and touched the ground. Larry, her fence lizard, crawled up her arm. Made me shiver.

"I better get going, too," Lizzy said. "Mr. and Mrs. Barker are going out on their Friday night date. Isn't that too cute! Mr. Barker rocks! I'll bet he brings her flowers."

The Barkers' oldest son was one of the few friends I'd made in Ashland, and Lizzy did a lot of babysitting for his five younger brothers.

"Tell Barker hey for me!" I called as Lizzy ran in the house.

I back-biked to Stable-Mart, pedaling backward to go frontward over scattered yellow, red, and brown leaves. The back bike looks like a regular bike, but Dad redid the gears and chains in reverse. It's just one of my dad's inventions, like the musical toaster or the electric shoehorn. At least I didn't have to ride *those* to school.

As I wheeled into the stable, I heard Bold Beauty's anxious snorts and the thud of her hooves echoing from the indoor arena. I raced to the end of the stalls, where I could watch without being spotted.

Summer Spidell shouted something at her brother as she galloped the mare toward a pole jump. She looked the part of an equestrian in jodhpurs and tall black boots, her long blonde hair tucked under a bowler. But her seat was off balance, and Beauty loped out of position.

Hawk walked up behind me. "She is magnificent."

"Hawk, they're ruining her! Look! Summer's going to clip that jump."

Sure enough, Summer leaned so far forward that the horse took off too soon. Front and back hooves ticked the pole, knocking it down. Summer jerked the reins, using them as lifelines.

"Coward can't jump, Richard!" Summer cried, trotting over to her brother. "This is a waste of time!"

"Coward?" I repeated, anger surging through me. Summer was the coward. That's why the horse was losing confidence.

"Summer says the horse's real name is Howard's Lionhearted Lady," Hawk explained. "They're calling her Coward's Chickenhearted Baby."

I turned to Hawk. She looked great, as always. Her shiny black hair fell neatly to her waist, and the leather capris and buckskin shirt she wore made her look like a fashion model. But something was missing, and I couldn't figure out what. . . .

Then I got it. "Where's Peter Lory?" Hawk's exotic red bird, a chattering lory, usually rides on her shoulder everywhere. She'd named her pet after an actor, Peter Lorre, who played gangsters in really old movies before they invented color.

Hawk's expression almost never gives away what she's thinking. But this time her forehead wrinkled and her eyes glistened. "I had to leave him at Pat's Pets until we get back from Europe."

Hawk's lawyer parents were taking her to check out a fancy boarding school in Paris. "Pat will take great care of Peter," I said. "I'll check on him, too. And *you* get to miss a week of classes!"

Hawk stared off into space. "I do not want to attend a boarding school."

"So tell them, Birdbrain!" I meant it as a joke. Hawk's totally into birds.

"For your information—" her words came out round, each one separated from the next "—many birds have remarkable brains. Chicka-dees, for example, hide thousands of seeds for winter and then grow new areas of the brain to remember where the seeds are. Scientists are studying *bird brains.*"

"I just meant you should be honest with your parents. You can tell them straight-out how you feel," I explained. "It's like jumping horses—all a matter of confidence!"

A scuffling sound came from the arena.

I sneaked closer for a better look. Sawdust and bright lights gave the Spidell indoor arena the look of a horse show. The ring was the only thing I envied at Stable-Mart, but I'd lose the bright lights and make the corners horse-friendly.

Summer swore at her brother, dismounted, and reset the pole jump she'd just botched.

Richard climbed into the saddle and yanked the reins so hard I could see the mare salivate.

"Richard's worse than Summer!" I complained to Hawk. I wanted to scream for him to stop.

He headed for the same jump Summer had nicked.

As he cantered past us, I whispered to Hawk, "The stirrups are too short. He rides too far back anyway!"

Beauty pricked her ears forward, then back, the way horses do to take in their surroundings. But Richard tightened the reins and dug his heels into her ribs as they approached the jump. She *had* to be confused.

I squeezed my eyes shut and rubbed the scar at my elbow, a horseshoe-shaped souvenir from the car accident that killed my mom. I couldn't bear to watch what I knew would be a lousy jump.

Thu-dump. Thu-dump. Thu-dump. Then a silence.

I opened my eyes in time to see the rough landing. Beauty stumbled. Richard jerked her head up and plopped hard in the saddle.

"I can't stand it!" I whispered.

"Winnie!" Hawk warned. "Don't—!"

But I was already storming the arena.

Bold Beauty nickered when she saw me, her soft brown eyes pleading with me not to make things worse. God must have planted that look because instead of losing my temper—and my job—I stopped and stroked Beauty's foaming neck, turned a darker red from sweat. I inhaled the horse scent that never fails to calm me down.

"Take her in and clean her up!" Richard shouted, dismounting. "Her owners are coming by later."

I stared at Richard as he yanked off his bowler and ran his fingers through his sandy blond hair. Lizzy says girls in high school are dying to go out with him, but I don't see why. Richard Spidell is the kind of guy who would lead a horse to water and *make* him drink. If Summer is a chip off the old, hard-hearted Spidell block, Richard is a chunk.

"Glad to help, Richard," I said, doing my best

to sound convincing. If I wanted him to let me train Beauty, I'd have to get on his good side . . . if he *had* a good side.

He straightened to his full, nearly six-foot height and narrowed his eyes at me. "'Glad to help'?"

Summer sidled up to her brother, their suspicious expressions a perfect match. "I know what you're thinking, Winnie. And the answer is *no*," said Summer.

Richard looked from Summer to me and back. "What's she thinking?"

Summer sighed. "Winifred Willis thinks she can do better with this *coward* of a horse than we can. You know what a great horse whisperer she thinks she is."

I glanced back at Hawk for support. She nodded for me to go for it . . . but *she* stayed put.

"Look, Richard . . ." I chose to ignore Summer. "Give me a chance with the mare. I'll work her until she gets her confidence back. You don't even have to tell the owners—"

"Who do you think you are?" Richard demanded.

Summer laughed, a cross between a giggle

and a cackle . . . a gackle. "If Richard and I can't get this horse to jump, *you* sure can't!" She sneered at me, then eyed her big brother. "Shouldn't Winifred be shoveling manure or something?"

Richard snatched Beauty's reins out of my hand so hard my palm stung. "Summer can groom Coward here. You better get those stalls cleaned if you want to keep your job."

I watched them walk off with Bold Beauty in tow. My throat burned. How could two people I think so little of make me feel so rotten?

"Sorry, Winnie," Hawk said as I hurried past her and went into the barn.

I pulled on rubber boots and went to work, stabbing the spade into a pile of manure. *This isn't over, Spidells! You can treat me like Cinderella and send me off to sweep cinders. But I'm going to rescue Bold Beauty if it takes a giant pumpkin and a fairy godmother to do it!*

$\mathcal{M}$issed a spot!" Summer leaned over the stall door and pointed.

I'd already mucked eight stalls and had almost finished this one, which belonged to Summer's American Saddle Horse, Spidell's Sophisticated Scarlet Lady. I'd kept her horse in the stall with me on purpose, even though the high-strung "Scar," my name for her, couldn't be trusted. Summer wouldn't have lasted two minutes in the stall with her nervous mare, and she knew it. Which is why I did it.

Scar kicked up wood shavings and paced. She'd been trying to bite me whenever my back was turned.

Like owner, like horse.

"I said," Summer shouted, "you missed a spot!"

"Thanks, Summer," I replied sweetly, flipping a spadeful of manure over my shoulder so she had to jump out of the way.

"You did that on purpose!"

I leaned on the spade. "Gorgeous *and* smart?"

Summer didn't know how to take that one. She twirled a strand of her long blonde hair. "Adrianna and Jeffrey Howard, of the Cleveland and Philadelphia Howards, are coming to ride their hunter. Be gone before they get here. *I* have to go jump."

Good idea. Take a flying leap.

She strode back to Bold Beauty in the arena. As far as I could tell, Summer still hadn't unsaddled the poor horse.

Hawk had gone home to pack for Europe, so I really was alone.

Now what am I supposed to do, God? You can't possibly want to leave your beautiful creation out there in the hands of Summer and her brother!

I'd been talking more to God lately. I still didn't pray like Lizzy did. She talked to God natural as sundown. But I'd come a long way since giving God the silent treatment after Mom died.

I shoved my braid off my shoulder and went

back to mucking. I'd just unloaded the last bucket of manure when I heard Richard yell, "They're here!"

I waited for Richard to run outside and greet his customers. Then I sneaked to the arena to watch.

When he came back, Richard wore a smile as broad as a Quarter Horse's rump. "Mr. and Mrs. Howard, my dad's sorry he couldn't be here today. This is my sister, Summer. We thought having her ride your mare would help get it used to a woman. It's your wife's horse, right?"

"My wedding gift to Adrianna." The handsome, dark-haired man put his arm around his pretty, auburn-haired wife. So they were newlyweds. "That horse won blue ribbons in hunt competition last year. I had no way of knowing she'd start refusing high jumps." Husband and wife wore matching brown jodhpurs and checkered jackets, like Barbie and Ken at the hunt.

Mrs. Howard snuggled closer and slipped her arm around his waist. "I love her, Jeffrey. I just hope I'm good enough for her." She smiled at Richard. "Jeffrey's parents belong to a hunt club. I love to ride and jump. But I have a lot to learn before I hunt at their level, I'm afraid."

"My wife's being modest. She's a wonderful rider!"

Sometimes I try to figure what kind of horse a person might be if people were horses. I could picture Jeffrey Howard as a Thorough-bred, with centuries of good breeding behind him. Mrs. Howard, too—or maybe even an Arabian, with a fine, light-bone structure and a natural grace.

I'd expected to write them off as rich snobs. But watching them, I couldn't lump them in with the Spidells. They kept looking at each other like they had to check to be sure the other one was still there and okay.

I tried to imagine my parents as newlyweds. I remembered running to the car once and catching them kissing. I'd pretended not to see.

Lizzy had said just a week after Mom died, "I miss *us*." She'd only been nine. I'd missed us, too, the four of us. I'd missed Mom and me. I'd even missed Lizzy and Mom and me. Now a new ache set in. I missed *them*. Not just my mom and dad. *Them*. Mr. and Mrs. Willis.

How many more ways could there be to miss Mom?

"Could I have a minute?" Richard tilted his

head, signaling to Mr. Howard that he wanted to talk in private.

His wife took the hint and lifted the reins from Summer. "Let me walk her a bit and get us used to each other."

"She's pretty lively!" Summer called after her.

Beauty tested Mrs. Howard, trying to stride ahead.

When they passed my hiding place, I ducked under the fence and fell in beside Beauty. "She likes to be scratched." Beauty stopped, and I reached up and scratched her withers. "Don't you, Beauty?"

"Beauty?" Adrianna Howard moved long, reddish fingernails to the withers.

"I call her Bold Beauty."

"I like that." She smiled and stuck out her hand. "I'm Adrianna."

"Winnie." I shook her hand. "You got yourself a great horse. A born hunter."

"Do you think so?" She eyed the mare.

"Look at her legs!" I explained. "I never saw any set truer—'one at each corner,' my mom used to say. And her eyes are kind and far apart, like her ears." I stopped talking. I'm usually lousy talking to people. Give me a horse any day. But

I didn't trust what Richard might be telling Adrianna's husband about Beauty.

Adrianna listened to me, not clearing her throat like a lot of people do the first time they hear me talk. I sound a little hoarse all the time. Lizzy says she wishes she had my voice. She'd be a newscaster.

"I told Jeffrey I'll never foxhunt," Adrianna whispered. "They drag hunt at the club."

I knew what that was. The hounds are trained to follow a fake scent instead of a live fox. They use a bag of aniseed, or even human scent, and drag a line for the hounds to follow. Riders get a faster ride than with a real fox, taking natural jumps in a wide-open field. But the dogs just get a reward at the end of the hunt. They don't get a fox. I was glad she and Beauty wouldn't be part of that.

"Adrianna?" Her husband waved her over. "Richard says they're making great progress. Do you want to ride and see for yourself?"

"Great!" She started off, then turned back and grinned at me. "Wish me luck!"

She was a good rider. Her husband said so himself. And Beauty was a sweet horse. Still, my chest thumped. The way Summer and Richard had been riding the mare, anything could happen.

"Adrianna!" I called. "Be careful when you—"

"Winifred!" Richard glared at me, his face like rock-hard ice. But the ice melted into a warm smile when he turned back to Jeffrey. "Winnie cleans stalls for us. Sorry for the interruption."

I felt my face heat up. Again I was Cinderella of the muck.

Fine. Beauty could clear any jump in that arena if she had the right rider. Maybe Adrianna would have the confidence Beauty needed.

Adrianna mounted. I liked her easy position in the saddle, legs hanging down straight, hands just above the withers. She posted, moving up and down with Beauty's high-stepping trot as they circled the arena.

Her husband hadn't exaggerated when he bragged about her riding. In a trot, diagonal pairs of front and hind legs move together, giving the bounciest gait. Adrianna made it look easy, rising from the saddle, moving forward slightly, supporting herself with her knees, and easing back into the saddle.

I relaxed, realized I'd been rubbing my horse-shoe scar, and stopped.

They headed toward the lowest jump, a pole resting low on two uprights, like a miniature goal. Adrianna headed her horse in straight, still at a trot, and allowed the mare to pace herself.

That's it. Aim her right, and she'll jump herself!

Beauty trotted without hesitation and eased over the pole, landing in a canter, as if the jump had been no more than the start of her faster gait.

Adrianna scratched Beauty's withers and kept cantering. I liked this rich woman more every minute.

She took the next two hurdles without fault, pressing her knees lightly against the saddle, heels down, toes pointing forward, shifting her weight to center of balance as they jumped. Bold Beauty loved it!

They did the next jump and the next. Adrianna didn't even have to adjust the pace. Only the high jump remained. They circled and prepared to take the hurdle.

Summer ran out. "Don't do that one!"

Adrianna slowed to a trot and pulled off course.

"What's the matter?" Jeffrey asked.

I could tell Richard was flustered. He tried to

24

get his friendly mask back on, but it didn't fit. His lips twitched. "Summer, get out of the way!"

Adrianna and Beauty walked up to them. "We were doing great! Why did you stop us?"

"Your horse won't take that high jump!" Summer snapped, ignoring her brother's glare.

I wondered if Summer cared about Adrianna's safety, or if she just couldn't stand getting shown up.

Jeffrey wheeled on Richard. "You said the horse was making progress."

"Summer had trouble with that jump." Richard forced a dry laugh. "Your horse *is* making progress."

"So it's okay then?" Adrianna asked, stroking Beauty's neck.

Summer's eyes narrowed to slits. "Fine! Go right ahead." As she stormed past me, she muttered, "I'm a better rider than she is any day!"

Adrianna cantered Beauty around the arena. As they thundered past me, I sensed tension in both of them. The gait seemed choppy, hooves shuffling instead of landing clean. Beauty's muscles had tightened, anticipating the jump. Adrianna looked stiffer, too, her elbows close to her sides, as if protecting herself. She held the reins closer to her chest, killing her freedom and Beauty's.

I couldn't swallow as I watched them head for the high hurdle. I knew it was about the height of my hedge in the pasture, but it appeared taller now, like a fortress wall.

Confidence! You both need to believe you can make it!

Beauty galloped faster toward the jump. *Thu-dump! Thu-dump! Thu-dump!* The horse was rushing it. The fourth stride landed too far away; the fifth would have put her in the pole. She lunged at it, lifted her head, tried to jump, changed her mind, twisted in the air, and came down on the approach side of the hurdle, bumping it with her nose. Her rider, already half out of the saddle, flew off.

"Adrianna!" Jeffrey's scream echoed as he raced to his wife.

The only sound cutting off his cry was the *thud* as Adrianna's body crashed to the ground.

Adrianna! Are you all right? Don't move."
Jeffrey knelt and threw his arms around his wife.

I got there a second after he did. "You okay?
Good landing!" She'd rolled and taken the brunt
of the fall on her arm.

Adrianna started to answer, but her husband
pulled her head against him so she couldn't.

"It's all my fault!" he cried. "I never should
have let you on that horse! I don't know what
I would have done if—"

Adrianna managed to pull away and get to
her feet. Her hat was still on and, except for
sawdust on her side, she looked fine. "I'm okay.
Is Beauty all right?"

"We should go to the hospital!" Jeffrey

insisted, the concern in his eyes so strong I had to look away.

Adrianna's husband was this upset, and *he* knew horses. No wonder Mom hadn't wanted Dad to know about her falls. He couldn't have handled it.

At the far end of the arena Bold Beauty galloped back and forth, dodging Summer's and Richard's attempts to catch her.

Richard gave up and ran over to us. He was breathing hard. "I'm afraid you made a bad mistake buying that horse for your wife."

Jeffrey drew his wife closer. "That mare was so reliable! Maybe something's wrong with her."

"We had the vet check her out," Richard explained. "He ran blood tests, but she's not anemic. No virus, no muscle problem." He glanced at Summer, who was lunging at Beauty, trying to catch her and not coming close. "So that leaves one answer. Your horse is a born stopper."

Anyone who jumps horses knows that's the death warrant for a hunter. Some horses are born stoppers and will refuse fences or a certain fence no matter what you do to them. But Beauty wasn't like that.

"She's not a stopper!" I shouted. "She's a born hunter. She loves to jump!"

Jeffrey turned to me as if I'd come up through the sawdust. His gaze landed on my mucking boots.

Richard snorted. "Winnie loves horses, don't you, Winnie?" He said it like I was five, used to playing with plastic horses.

"I have to be honest with you," Richard said, man-to-man to Jeffrey. "You're wasting your money training this horse. Why don't you let me find a more suitable hunter for your wife? There's a riding school in Cleveland that would take this one off your hands. Leave it to me."

"Richard!" Summer screamed from the other end of the arena. She kicked the ground, spraying sawdust. "*You* catch this beast!"

Richard smiled patiently at the Howards. The perfect big brother. "Excuse me, will you? This won't take a minute."

He marched over to Summer and whispered something that made her stiffen.

"I did, you idiot!" Summer screamed. "*You* try! See how great *you* do!"

Richard shot a fake, nervous smile at us. If I

hadn't been so worried about Bold Beauty,
I might have enjoyed this scene.

Summer, hands on hips, glared at her
brother as he walked toward the horse. Beauty
let him get within a horse's tail length. Then
she pivoted away. He came again. She backed
up. He grabbed for her, and she took off at a
gallop.

"If you're sure you're all right," Jeffrey said, his
hands on his wife's shoulders, "I'll go give him a
hand."

"Go! I'm fine." Adrianna watched her husband jog over to Richard and Summer. "This is
all my fault. Beauty really is a sweet horse."

"And you can't sell her!" I pleaded.

"That will be up to Jeffrey. It's his gift. He
knows more about hunters than I do."

"She's just lost her confidence here. Couldn't
you feel it? She was smooth and sure over all
the jumps until that last one."

"When I doubted her," Adrianna admitted.

"All she needs is a good rider to give her back
her confidence! She already knows how to
jump. *I* could ride her!" There. I'd said it. No
sense stopping now. "I can get her to jump that
high jump. I know it!"

Adrianna raised her eyebrows. "But I thought you didn't work horses here."

"But I *could!* If you said you wanted me to train Beauty, they'd have to let me. I've gentled other horses, honest!"

At the other end of the arena, Beauty had all three humans—Richard, Summer, and Jeffrey—running in circles.

"Richard seems awfully sure about the horse," Adrianna said.

"But he doesn't love horses!" I insisted. "Not like I do."

Adrianna narrowed her green eyes. They seemed to see inside me. "I do know how you feel about horses, Winnie. You already love my horse, don't you?"

I nodded. "And I've never met a horse I couldn't fix." It sounded like bragging, even to me. But it was the truth.

Adrianna grinned. "I believe you. And if it's confidence that horse needs, you certainly seem loaded with it."

Jeffrey came dragging back. "We can't catch her. I think Richard's right. We're better off selling her and letting him find you a proper hunter."

"Richard's wrong!" I blurted out.

"Jeffrey," Adrianna said sweetly, "Winnie thinks she can help. She trains horses, too."

He squinted at me and my boots again.

"I know I don't look like much. But I'm almost 13." My birthday wasn't for another six months, but I threw that in since most people think I'm younger. "And I've had experience with jumpers. In Wyoming." I wished Lizzy were here. She could have talked them into it. "Please give me a chance!"

Jeffrey shook his head. "I'm sorry. I don't think—"

Richard rushed over. "The mare's too excited now. We'll get some help and catch her later."

I got an idea. I turned to Jeffrey. "*I'll* catch her."

Richard laughed.

He shouldn't have laughed. He'd seen me catch wild horses before.

"Look," I reasoned, "if I can catch her, will you give me a chance to train her?"

"You?" Richard sounded like I'd just asked to be crowned Miss America.

"I think that's fair," Adrianna agreed, flashing me a smile.

I took that as a yes, knowing it was as close as I'd get to one, and hurried out to Bold Beauty.

I passed Summer in the middle of the arena. "Don't tell me. You're going to catch her. Big deal!"

Summer was right. I'd need to do more than catch a horse to convince Jeffrey to give me a chance with Beauty. Richard had him convinced the horse was a lost cause and I was Cinderella of the Stables. Even if I caught Beauty, Richard would say it was luck or they'd tired her out for me.

I had to convince them I knew what I was doing. "Easy, girl," I called as I approached the mare.

She snorted and pawed the ground.

I eased my arms out from my sides, forming a *T* with my body. I stared directly at her, an aggressive move in horse language. "Don't you dare come to me!" I called. "Get moving."

I stepped toward her, forcing her into a trot away from me. I stayed angled on her, making her trot in a circle around me. "That's right. I didn't say you could come in yet, did I?"

She broke into a canter but stayed to the circle, eyeing me, bobbing her head.

Still facing Beauty, I called back to the Howards. "Ever notice how, when you go into a pasture filled with horses, they all come to you except the one you want to catch?" My voice sounded raspier than usual. I swallowed.

"That's exactly right!" Adrianna laughed.

"It's not a coincidence. You're only trying to catch that one, and horses don't like to be caught. In fact, you should never try to catch a horse. Instead, let the horse catch you. That's what I'm doing here. I'm making Beauty want to catch me, to *join up*."

"We don't have time for this!" Richard objected. But I didn't hear any of them leave.

I kept Beauty trotting. "Not yet," I told her. "Not yet, girl."

After a minute, her head lowered. Then I saw what I was waiting for. She licked her lips. In horse language, that means *Can I come in and hang out with you?*

I lowered my arms and looked away from her. "Come on in now. Good girl."

Bold Beauty walked straight to me. I scratched her withers. Without taking her reins, I turned my back and joined the others. Beauty followed at my shoulder all the way over.

"Bravo!" Adrianna cried. "Well done!"

"Not bad," Jeffrey admitted, his lips curving into a grin.

"So you'll let me train her? Two weeks. That's all I need. I'll have her sailing over that high hurdle—"

"She can't train here!" Summer cried.

"Winnie doesn't work horses here!" Richard roared. "I can't allow it."

I glared at them. It wasn't fair. They didn't want Beauty—or me—to have a chance. I knew if I asked their dad, he'd say the same thing. "I can train her in my pasture! There's even a hedge the same height as that high jump!"

"Really?" Adrianna turned to her husband. "We could loan her our cavalletti!" She pointed to the pole jump and the stack of red-and-white poles to the side.

I'd know what to do with them. Mom had used cavalletti poles to work with jumpers in Wyoming.

"I don't know . . ." Jeffrey looked at his wife.

"Jeffrey, if there's any chance Beauty could work out, I think it's worth a try. We could leave her while we're on our honeymoon."

Jeffrey put his arm around her and turned to

me. "My wife is impossible to argue with. We're leaving tonight. Can you bring your trailer and pick up the mare?"

Yes!

Summer laughed. "Her trailer? The day Winnie gets a trailer, I'll get a spaceship and fly to Venus!"

Note to self: Get a trailer.

"You won't be sorry! You'll see!" I couldn't believe it. They were going to let me train her! "And I'll just ride Beauty home!" I started to mount. My mucking boots barely fit into the metal stirrups.

"Ride her? On streets?" Adrianna asked.

"She's traffic shy. Since she started refusing jumps, she's scared of everything," Jeffrey explained.

I swung up into the saddle. She had to be at least 17½ hands high, two hands taller than Nickers. "Then I'll cure her traffic shyness, too."

"Didn't I tell you she had enough confidence for all of us?" Adrianna stood on tiptoes and handed me her hat.

"Two weeks then," Jeffrey said. "We'll pay you what we were paying Spidells, if that's all right. Half the monthly fee?"

I gulped. Half the Spidell fee was four times

what I charged Hawk to keep Towaco. With that much money, I wouldn't have to muck Spidells' stalls all winter. "Great!"

I rode out of the stable and down the long driveway. *God, thanks for giving them confidence in me.*

The stirrups were too long, or my legs too short. It had been a couple of years since I'd ridden a hunt saddle, and it felt weird—light, like English saddles, but deep-seated, with padded knee rolls. Give me bareback any day.

Beauty still wore the sheepskin-lined leather tendon boots that protected her from clipping her front feet with her hind hooves. The boots clumped along as she pranced down the road.

The Howards drove by in a silver car and waved. Beauty tensed, but didn't bolt.

The orange sun hung low, leaving the air chilled and tuning up a chorus of crickets. I felt like jumping over the sun and almost believed I could. Beauty raised each hoof too high, springing from the road, flicking her ears at a woodpecker, snorting at falling leaves. Behind us, a horn honked.

Beauty stopped, her legs stiff, every muscle coiled.

"Easy," I murmured, scratching her withers.

Richard pulled up beside us in his new black Mustang convertible. "We don't appreciate you stealing clients!"

"You'd given up on this horse, Richard! What was I supposed to do?"

"Well, you're fired!"

"I quit!"

He gunned the engine, squealing tires, spraying gravel and dust.

Beauty reared, then bolted sideways. I tried to get her back on the road. But her hooves slid on the grass. Her hind legs scrambled.

"Whoa!"

She couldn't whoa. We slid toward the ditch in slow motion. Right fore and hind foot plunged down the ditch. And, like a plastic horse knocked on its side, Beauty toppled over.

$\mathcal{M}$y elbow brushed the ground, but I managed to stay in the saddle. Beauty and I were practically lying on the side of the ditch.

"Easy," I murmured.

I thought I heard someone calling my name. But I couldn't look. It was all I could do to stay on.

Beauty thrust her head forward. With a lunge, she stumbled up and out of the ditch. My heart pounded. Beauty shook herself off like a dog coming out of a pond.

"Man, you okay?" Catman Coolidge hopped off his back bike, Dad's first sale. Catman's blond hair flowed behind him, and his wire-rimmed glasses scooted down his nose.

I don't think I'd ever seen Catman un-calm

before. He's so cool, a throwback to the 60s. He looks like a hippie in an old movie about protests and flower children.

Catman touched my muck boot, as if he didn't care how dirty it was. "Bummer about the fall!"

I felt like crying. It might have been from Beauty's close call . . . or because I didn't know Catman cared so much. He was probably the best friend I had, although neither of us would have said so. I hated that he'd seen me almost fall.

"I'm still on," I pointed out. "And in one piece. Meet Bold Beauty. I'm training her to jump."

"Already pretty jumpy." He retrieved his bike and turned it around to head in my direction. "That's a lot of horse, Winnie."

The last thing I wanted was for Catman to doubt me as a horse gentler. "She's *not* too much horse for me. Mom told me about a horse foaled in England over 150 years ago, a Shire gelding that measured $21\frac{1}{2}$ hands. That's almost $7\frac{1}{2}$ feet tall."

"Maybe the trainer stood over five feet." He was teasing. I *am* over five feet. But I knew he didn't totally believe I could handle Beauty.

As I rode home with Catman walking his bike beside us, I filled him in on the details. "I've got two weeks to get Beauty over the high jump. I'll bet I could get her to take that big hedge right now if I wanted to."

"Pretty sure of yourself for a cat who just came out of a ditch."

"I am! And that's what Beauty needs. Nine times out of 10, a bad jump is the rider's fault. If the rider loses confidence, so will her horse."

"I'm hip."

As we walked, cats fell in behind us. Burg, a.k.a. Cat Burglar, one of Catman's brood, crept out from a bush, his black mask ruffled against his white fur. Churchill, a big, flat-faced cat, trudged along with Nelson, my barn cat. Four kittens darted out of a ditch. Catman was the pied piper of cats in Ashland, Ohio.

"Wilhemina!" Catman called.

Wilhemina is a fat orange tabby, named after the author Charles Dickens' cat. She plodded up behind us just as a pickup approached ahead of us.

Beauty froze, nostrils flaring. She jerked sideways, but I held her to the road. The truck passed us slowly, and I felt her relax.

Catman shook his head at Beauty.

"I told the Howards I'd cure her of shying, too," I admitted.

He glanced up at me. "You got that kind of time?"

Why didn't he understand how good I am with horses? He'd seen me gentle my own horse, Nickers, and several other horses, too. But I guess Catman Coolidge was hard to impress.

When we reached my house, Catman beeped his bike horn. But instead of a beep, out came a sound like a rush of wind, a tornado.

Beauty shied, then kept walking.

"Catman, what did you do to your horn?" Before it had meowed, thanks to Dad's invention, the cat horn.

Catman grinned his catlike grin. "Your dad's idea. He figured out what they used for the tornados in that movie *Twister*."

"What is it?" I asked.

"Camel. I went to the Cleveland Zoo and recorded a camel moaning."

Note to self: Never go to the zoo with Catman.

Catman and his cats hung out with me in the barn. When Dad first rented our house from Pat

Haven, he hadn't even known we'd be getting a barn thrown in. The building needed paint and a few repairs, but I loved the smell of horse and fresh hay and the way light poked through knots in the barn wood. Nickers loved her home, too.

I cooled Beauty down and introduced her to Towaco and Nickers. I'd planned on getting the three together slowly. But Nickers surprised me by being a good hostess and making up fast. Usually, she's as lousy with horses as I am with people.

Catman and I crossed the lawn, littered with "works-in-progress" people had dropped off for my dad, Odd-Job Willis, to fix. Dad can fix anything from radios to washing machines, but he'd rather work on his inventions. He claims that even in his insurance days he dreamed of becoming an inventor. He just never had time to work on stuff.

Dad stopped hammering and waved. "Catman! Come see this!"

"Hey, Dad!" I shouted, knowing he didn't mean to ignore me. He just gets so wrapped up in his inventions. And Catman had been helping him.

We headed for the pile of wood Dad was working on.

"Stop!" Lizzy dropped from a tree and threw herself in front of us. "Don't take another step!"

"Lizzy—," I started.

"Can't you see what you're walking into? There!" She pointed, but I didn't see anything.

"Far out!" Catman stared into space.

"It's an orb weaver, Catman!" Lizzy exclaimed. "I watched him weave it. He got interrupted twice, and each time he started over from scratch, like the whole weaving pattern was memorized but only if he started from the beginning."

I moved closer to Catman, and then I saw it. A fantastic web stretched between two trees, hundreds of thread-fine spokes crisscrossing circle after circle. I shuddered, glad I hadn't walked into it. "Where's the spider, Lizzy?"

"Waiting." She showed us where a fat, black spider lurked in the far corner of his web. "See how he holds onto the silk thread, waiting for something to land? He feels the vibration and pounces! This afternoon he caught a wasp!"

"Cool." Catman got so close to the web I was afraid his nose would touch and the spider would pounce. "So, you got tired of lizards?"

"Catman!" Lizzy scolded. "Never! How could I? I love all 3,000 species of lizards! Don't I, Larry?"

Larry the Lizard stuck his head out of Lizzy's pants pocket, and Lizzy petted him. "Besides, I could never collect spiders. They don't make friends like lizards do. Put two spiders in a box, and they'll fight to the death!"

"Catman!" Dad yelled.

"Stay for dinner, Catman," Lizzy urged. "I made a spider-shaped casserole that rocks!"

"I can dig it." Catman ducked under the web.

"Tell me about the new horse, Winnie," Lizzy said as we watched Catman join Dad and immediately drop to the ground to inspect some new invention.

I explained to Lizzy how I'd ended up with Bold Beauty and how I'd be jumping her.

"I'd love to get a jumping spider!" Lizzy exclaimed. "They're so cute! Two huge eyes in the middle, four more on top, and one on each side. They don't even have to move their heads to see everywhere. And can they jump! Of course, fleas are better jumpers. They can jump 150 times their length, which is like us jumping over a 100-story building! Spiders can't jump that high, but . . ."

I rolled my eyes at my sister, then joined Catman and Dad by what looked more like a rocking chair than one of Dad's crazy inventions.

"Congratulations on getting another horse to gentle, Winnie!" Dad handed Catman a screwdriver. "Catman said it's a jumper?"

"A hunter actually." I liked that Catman had told Dad about it—and that he *hadn't* mentioned the run-in with the ditch. "Great pay, too. I won't have to clean Stable-Mart stalls anymore." No sense wasting time on the details of that one.

"Uh-huh." Dad pushed the rocker back and forth.

"Are you making chairs, Dad?"

"Like no, man!" Catman was screwing a tube-line rod to the back of the chair. "Your dad's inventing the first rocker-powered fan!"

"Rocket-powered—?" I repeated.

"*Rocker*-powered!" Catman corrected. "Dude sits and rocks. Then energy—"

Dad interrupted, continuing as if they had one brain, forming the same sentence. "—transfers through air, which is sucked up into this

tube to a generator fan!" He sat in the chair
and rocked. "Air up. It blows through the fan—
we're still working on that—turns the blades.
Voila! Fan blows on the rocker! No electricity!
No battery!"

"Rocker-powered," I muttered.

At least it was a step up from the toaster that
buttered toast on the way out . . . or the electric
fork . . . or the boomerang baseball . . . or the
automatic cat comb. Even Catman didn't like
that one.

I cleaned up, and Lizzy finished cooking
dinner while I set the table for four. We didn't
get much company, so it felt strange to fill the
little kitchen table. It made me think about
Mom and dinners when we had always set the
table for four.

During dinner Lizzy did most of the talking,
and most of it about spiders. "Of course, not all
spiders use webs to catch dinner. Some jump on
their prey. Others spit out sticky nets of poison
and trap anything in their paths. But spitters live
mainly indoors, so—"

"Lizzy!" Dad gulped a mouthful of spider-
shaped casserole. "Could we please change the
subject?"

Good. I wanted the subject to turn to Bold Beauty and me.

But before I could jump in, Catman spoke. "I brought those entry forms, Mr. W."

I glanced at Lizzy, but she shrugged. "What entry forms?" I asked.

"Nothing." Dad shook his head. "Catman, I told you I didn't think I'd have the rocker ready in time."

"In time for what?" Lizzy asked.

"The Inventor's Contest," Catman said. "Winner gets a trip to the Invention Convention in Chicago."

Dad shoved his plate away. "I'd never win something like that with one of my inventions. Real inventors enter those contests."

"You should do it!" Lizzy exclaimed. "That would be so great if you won! Do inventor kids get to go? Sweet! I have friends in Chicago from—what grade was I in there? Oh, it doesn't matter. When is it?"

Dad stood up. "I'm not entering. I have to make some calls."

Dad left, and we sat there finishing our dinner. I figured it was Dad's business whether he entered the contest or not.

Lizzy broke the silence, as usual. "So, Winnie, will this new horse be hard to gentle?"

"You should have seen that cat on the road, shying at her own shadow," Catman said, meaning horse. "Winnie's got her hands full." He turned to me. "She thinks she can make that cat road-safe."

I forced myself to sound as cool as Catman. "I'll cure her of shying tomorrow." I yawned for effect. "You're welcome to come watch if you like."

"In one day?" Catman almost sounded impressed.

Mom taught me that horses shy for one of five reasons: boredom, habit, orneriness, terror, or lack of confidence. Finding out *why* a horse shies is half the battle. I already knew why Beauty shied—lack of confidence.

"One day," I promised.

Catman narrowed his Siamese-blue cat eyes at me. "This I gotta see."

$\mathcal{S}$aturday I woke to honking and made it to my window in time to see a crooked *V* of Canadian geese fly over the barn. I pulled on jeans and a sweatshirt and dashed through the dewy grass for an early ride on Nickers.

As we cantered around the pasture, an autumn, apple smell filled my lungs. Greens blurred into yellow and orange. Shaded maples clung to summer, with only their tips turned red—like autumn fingernails. I eyed the hedge as we galloped by, imagining Beauty and me flying over it.

When I finished with Nickers, I took a spin on Towaco, making sure he didn't forget his leads before Hawk came back.

Then it was Bold Beauty's turn. I'd just started brushing the mud off her back when Catman appeared, wearing striped bell-bottoms and a paisley shirt.

"Dirty," he commented.

"Hey, Catman! Dirt's good. Means Beauty felt at home enough to roll. Bet she never rolled at Stable-Mart."

Beauty craned her neck around to nuzzle me. I blew into her nostrils, an old Indian trick. Greet a horse the way they greet each other. Beauty blew back. I already felt myself getting too attached to her. But it would be okay. She'd be getting a good home. Adrianna wasn't just a good owner; she was a good rider. That helped.

"Saddle?" Catman asked.

"Thanks, but no thanks." I slipped on the bridle. Beauty opened her mouth for me and kept her head low. "Bareback."

"Nothing to hang on to," he observed.

"I don't need anything to hang on to." I swung myself onto her back. "I want to *feel* her. Horses have sensory cells running through their skin. When Mom and I watched this herd of Mustangs once, we couldn't believe how they kept touching and brushing against each other. But that's how they read moods and thoughts. Beauty and I need to feel each other."

"Cats don't need to touch you to know everything you're thinking . . . before you do." He set down Nelson, and the tiny black cat with one white paw pranced straight to Nickers' stall and pounced to the feed trough.

"Now *that's* a horse!" Eddy Barker, wearing his Cleveland Indians hat backward, strolled up as I rode Beauty out of the barn. He carried Chico, his brother Luke's Chihuahua. Next to Barker, whose skin is the color of a deep bay, the puppy looked snow-white. But their big, brown eyes matched.

"Hey, Barker!" I struggled to keep Beauty still.

Eddy Barker is about the nicest person I've ever met—and not dull nice either. He trains dogs, plays basketball even though he's not much taller than I am, and I don't know if I've ever seen him without the big smile he turned on me now. "Did Pat get hold of you?"

Pat Haven runs the pet shop where Catman, Barker, and I work on the computer Pet Help Line. She'd been subbing in life science since the first day of school, since the teacher we were supposed to have said he had to go out and "find himself" or something.

"Nope. Why?" I pulled lightly on the reins, and Beauty backed up until I released.

"The debate." Barker snapped on a leash and set Chico down.

"Barker, I told you a hundred times! I'm not volunteering for those debates until they make me." Pat had made a Life Science assignment that everybody in her class had to debate one topic before the semester ended. Pat coached one side, and our English teacher, Ms. Brumby, coached the other. They claimed they wanted to make us think about stuff. Kids were supposed to volunteer when a topic came along that interested them. So far my classmates had debated war and the environment. I was putting it off as long as possible.

"Come on, Winnie," Barker pressed. "Pat and I both want you on the abortion debate. You'll have to go with a topic sometime."

"Not if the school burns down or a tornado hits or snow . . ." I knew it didn't make any sense to hope the debate assignment would just go away, but it made even less sense to volunteer to make a total idiot of myself in front of everybody.

Barker glanced at Catman, then back at me.

"Winnie, this is the topic I've been waiting for. I know you're as pro-life as I am. This debate could actually make a difference."

"Barker, you've heard me in class. I was the one saying, 'Uh . . . um . . . duh . . .' You wouldn't want me on your team!"

"Count me in, man!" Catman held up his fingers in the peace sign. "Kids. Peace. Inside the womb and out."

"Thanks, Catman," Barker said. "But it's seventh grade only. No eighth-graders."

I reached down and untangled a lock of Beauty's mane. "Barker, I'll be cheering for you louder than anybody, but I just can't—"

Chico interrupted with yaps that should have come from a dog 10 times his size.

Bold Beauty jumped sideways.

"Sorry!" Barker scooped up the loudmouthed dog.

"That's okay." I circled Beauty until she calmed down. "I want to get Beauty used to everything. And that includes dogs."

"In one day." When Catman said it, it sounded like a challenge.

"One day." I rode in front of him. "So if you'll excuse me, I'm off."

"Ditto." Catman sniffed the air. "I smell biscuits and bacon."

Catman and Barker headed in for a Lizzy breakfast, while Beauty and I tiptoed through the maze of junk on our lawn.

Mom once posted a list in our barn in Wyoming: *Top 10 Spooky Objects for Horses.* My mind had taken one of its automatic pictures, and I could see the smudged white paper with blue lines and the swirls and slant of Mom's handwriting:

1. *Blowing paper*
2. *Barking dogs*
3. *Mud puddles*
4. *Trash cans*
5. *Little kids*
6. *Plaid horse blankets*
7. *Ropes and hoses on the ground*
8. *Ponies*
9. *Windy days*
10. *Wagons and trucks and cars*

Dad had conveniently supplied me with most of the Top 10 on our own junky lawn. For the next hour, I let Beauty walk around sniffing strange objects. Horses identify each other and size up their world by smell. Beauty snorted at a bent, metal trash can. I gave her time to soak up the information. Horses have an extra sense organ at the end of their long nasal passages. It's called the Jacobson's organ, and they use it to decide if objects are friends or enemies. Lizzy says snakes have the Jacobson's organ, too.

Beauty and I moved from plastic cords to cardboard to an old red wagon. Beauty sniffed and nuzzled, processing each fear and gaining confidence.

Lizzy came outside with the boys, and I showed them how well Beauty was behaving. When Chico barked, I told Barker to let him bark away. Beauty shied, but didn't take long to settle down.

"Not bad!" Barker shouted.

But I didn't just want Beauty confident. I wanted her overconfident. I rode closer to them. "Want to help?"

Lizzy grabbed Chico. "I'll help by getting this puppy . . . and me . . . . as far away from this as possible."

"Deal!" I couldn't risk Beauty smelling Lizzy's fear. I turned to Barker and Catman. "As for you guys, mount your bikes!"

Barker's bike was regular, although he claimed all the Barker boys had asked for back bikes for Christmas. He and Catman pedaled to the street while Beauty watched as intently as if they were tigers threatening to pounce.

I explained my plan as I urged Beauty into the street. "I want to teach Beauty that bikes are nothing to be afraid of. Ride slowly, and we'll tag along."

Beauty wasn't crazy about the idea, but she walked beside them as they coasted down our street.

"When I give the cue," I instructed, "you guys bike off fast."

Beauty pricked her ears as we trailed the bikes. She bobbed her head, but moved in behind them. When I could see yards ahead and no cars, I hollered, "Now!"

Barker and Catman took off, tires squealing.

Beauty broke into a trot.

"That's it, Beauty! They're scared of you! See how they're running away?"

Bold Beauty must have believed me. She broke into a canter and charged, kicking up her heels for fun. At last, *she* was the one chasing!

"Thanks!" I yelled. "Keep going!" I turned Beauty around and brought her down to a walk.

Behind us, I heard a car turn onto the street. *Here we go!*

I peeked over my shoulder and saw Pat Haven's little car. I waved Pat up beside us, and Beauty sidestepped. She wasn't cured yet.

Pat stuck her head out the window. Her brown curls coiled across her face. I expected to hear them go *boing, boing.* "So that's the new horse. Pretty. Doesn't seem like a scaredy-cat to me, no offense." Pat never failed to apologize for her animal expressions, even when the animal wasn't around.

I trotted, staying side by side with Pat's car. She was sitting on a pillow, hands gripping the steering wheel at ten and two o'clock. The road looked deserted except for us. "Could I ask you a favor, Pat?"

"And me coming to see you to ask *you* a favor. Isn't that the bee's knees! No offense. You first, sugar!"

"Would you drive slowly to the barn?" I asked. "When I raise my hand, speed up. I want Beauty to believe she's chasing you away."

"Well, I don't like deceiving a body. But if you

say so, I'll make an exception." She pulled in front of me, barely moving.

Beauty couldn't even trot without running into Pat's bumper. I waved my hand.

Pat sped up, and Beauty took to a trot. I waved my arm again until we were galloping behind Pat's car.

"Look at you!" I told Beauty. "You're scaring off that big ol' car!"

We "chased" Pat all the way to my house. I walked Beauty straight to the cross-ties and got her brushes.

Pat followed us in. "I can understand why a horse would be scared of a car. Big, ugly things—cars I mean."

"Well, Beauty won't be scared any longer," I said. "She thinks they're scared of her."

Pat frowned. "But they're not."

I laughed. "But Beauty *thinks* they are. That gives her confidence on the road."

Pat pinched a stray curl and let it *boing* against her temple. "But it's a false confidence. Sooner or later, won't she run up against a car she can't chase?"

She had a point, but I was feeling too good to get into it. Besides, I knew why she'd come.

Might as well get it over with. "Pat, I think I already know your favor. Barker dropped by earlier."

"Good!" she exclaimed. "This abortion debate should be the best one yet. I think it's the most important and—"

"Pat, I don't want to volunteer for the abortion debate." I kept brushing Beauty. "You've heard me talk in your class. I can't string four words together without messing one up, not in front of people."

"But we need you!" Pat protested. "Ms. Brumby is coaching the pro-choice side, with Summer, Brian, Kristine, and Grant."

"Grant's arguing for abortion?" I'd gotten to know Grant Baines when I trained his Quarter Horse. "I can't believe he thinks it's okay to end a life."

"Honey, I think most of the kids don't know what they believe. They haven't thought much about abortion *or* life." Pat sighed. "And I want them to think."

Talk about pressure. I could feel God pressing against my heart. "What about Andrew?" Andrew was one of the smartest kids in the whole school. When he talked, he sounded like a teacher.

Pat shook her head. "Andrew's waiting for the debate on animal rights. Our goose is cooked—no offense—if we can't get four people on the pro-life side. I promised the class I wouldn't force any topic on them. But I want this one, Winnie. And I want you."

"You don't want me, Pat! I'd get tongue-tied."

"Bosh! God can untie that tongue when it's saying what he wants!" Pat whipped out a carrot for Beauty, as if she just walked around with pocketfuls. Beauty chomped gratefully. "Pray about it, okay?"

Pat left, and I was about to take Beauty off the cross-ties when I glanced at my watch. Four o'clock. I hadn't ridden Beauty that hard. I'd gotten her over shying in less than a day. Why not try jumping?

I sensed Catman in the barn and turned to see him holding Nelson.

"You missed it, Catman! Beauty chased Pat's car! No more shying—in *less* than a day, thank you very much. And I'll bet her confidence carries over to jumping. In fact, I'll bet I could take her over the high jump right now."

A shiver of excitement ran through me. That would be so amazing! All Beauty needed was a rider with confidence, and I had it! "I'll do it," I muttered.

"Do what?" Catman asked.

"Take Bold Beauty over that hedge," I answered, already putting the bridle back on.

"Thought you had to train her first." Catman set down Nelson and walked over to Beauty.

My mind was racing. I imagined telling the Howards that I'd cured their horse—in 24 hours!

Catman tossed me the bowler, and I strapped it on. He stood at Beauty's left shoulder and cupped his hands for me to use as a stirrup. Beauty stood still for the mount, but her skin twitched as I settled into the curve behind her withers and gathered the reins in both hands. It was like she knew what was coming and wanted it as much as I did.

Beauty pranced to the pasture as if she hadn't been ridden in a month. We cantered around, taking two fallen logs without losing stride. *Winnie the Hunter Gentler.*

I looped and aimed for the hedge.

And Winnie Willis on the powerful Bold Beauty comes to the final jump with a perfect score. They look confident. The fans rise to their feet. Horse and rider gallop, challenging the hedge head-on! Stride, stride, stride!

Beauty snorted in time to her pounding hooves. High horsepower!

The hedge seemed to rush at us, as if *it* wanted to jump *us*.

Closer and closer.

Something felt wrong. The beat was off. Beauty raised her head against the reins, short-ened her stride. Her jaws opened. She wanted to stand back and fly at the hedge. But she was too far away.

She hesitated, then lunged. The unsteady surge of power jarred my bones. We soared in midair. But the hedge still lay under her nose. We'd never make it. I leaned forward, willing her over. The old horseman's saying popped into my head: *Throw your heart over the fence, and your horse will follow.*

But my heart clung to my ribs.

I heard her forelegs strike the hedge. Beauty's belly scraped as she skimmed over. She landed hard on her front hooves, stumbling to get her hind end clear of the monster hedge.

Beauty's knees buckled. With a jolt, I felt myself propelled from her back. Up . . . up . . .

and over her head I tumbled. Sky. Clouds.
Grass.

Then pain.

And total darkness.

When I opened my eyes, I couldn't see the sun. For an instant I thought I was blind. Then the dark circle blocking the sun came into focus. Catman stood over me, hovering so close his hair dangled against my cheek.

Light danced behind my eyeballs. My chest burned. I struggled for air.

Then it came. I gasped. Air rushed in, like cold water flushing my lungs.

Catman was saying something. "Winnie? You got the wind knocked out of you!"

"Beauty . . ." At least that's what I said inside my head. It came out a squeak, as if squeezed through me before popping out.

Catman frowned at me.

"Beauty?" I whispered.

Catman stood up. "She's cool."

I wanted to believe him. But lying flat on my back, I couldn't see her. And I was afraid to move. Like if I turned my head, I'd shatter.

Catman stepped away and came right back, holding Beauty's reins.

I looked up at the mare.

"See?" Catman scratched behind Beauty's ears.

Beauty lowered her head and nuzzled my neck. She blew in my face. It was all the wind I could muster to blow back at her. *Thank you, God. I couldn't have handled it if I'd hurt Beauty.*

Catman led her back and forth where I could see her. Her eyes looked bright. She didn't limp.

Mom had a rule about getting right back on a horse after a fall. But that wasn't going to happen. Beauty deserved to run free, away from stupid humans.

I bit my cheek to keep from crying. "I . . . have to . . . get the . . . bridle off." I pressed my hands to the ground to push myself up. Pain shot through my left shoulder. I lay back down.

"Winnie?" Catman sounded scared. "I'm clueing in your dad."

"No!" I shouted. "Please, Catman! He's not home anyway."

"Lizzy can get Doc."

"No! I landed on my shoulder. I'll be all right."

Catman reached up to Beauty's bridle, unbuckled the throat latch, and slipped the headstall over her ears. Beauty gave up the bridle, shook her head, turned, and cantered off.

I swallowed warm tears. I could handle the pain. My head didn't hurt. I'd have been screaming if I'd broken anything.

What I couldn't stand was what I'd done to Bold Beauty. How had it happened? I'd been so confident, so sure I could take that hedge.

Something soft brushed my face.

"Nickers!" She nuzzled my cheek, blowing warm air on my skin. "I'm okay, girl." I reached over with my right arm to scratch her cheek. She nickered, low and long. I'd never loved her more than I did right then, when I had no right to be loved by any horse.

"Winnie, what's the skinny?" Catman dropped cross-legged on the ground next to me, Nickers on one side, Catman on the other.

"I'm fine," I assured him. "Help me up, okay?"

When I sat up, the pasture spun in a quick circle, then stopped. Nickers lipped the top of my head.

Catman stared into my face and grinned. "Nice shiner."

My hand went to my tender cheekbone. I had a vague recollection of hitting myself in the face as I landed. *Great. A black eye. How do I explain that one?*

I wiggled my toes like they do in hospital shows on TV, then turned to Catman. "Nobody can know about this. Promise me!"

"Not cool, Winnie." Catman shook his head. "Somebody ought to scope you out. Your dad—"

"No! Mom kept lots of horse problems from Dad so he wouldn't worry! From Lizzy too!" I broke down into a shoulder-shaking cry that hurt my left shoulder and made me cry harder.

I hadn't wanted to cry like a baby in front of Catman. But the tears ended up doing what my words couldn't. He stuck both his hands in the air. "Chill. You win! Stop crying! I can't dig it, man!"

I wiped tears with the back of my hand. "Thanks, Catman."

Nobody could know I'd fallen, not even Lizzy. She was scared of horses already. And she'd never be able to keep her mouth shut around Dad. If he found out, he'd lose all confidence in me as a horse gentler. Besides, Dad had just started feeling settled in Ashland. He didn't need me to worry about.

For a few minutes, my jagged breaths and sniffs were all that passed between us.

"I won't tell—for now," Catman promised. "But I don't like it. And I want you to see my mother."

"Your mother?" Mrs. Coolidge worked in a beauty salon, not a hospital. "Why your mother?"

"Claire finished two years of nursing school before she found her true calling." Catman wheeled up his bike. "Handlebars," he commanded. He balanced his bike while I climbed sidesaddle on the bar in front of him.

Catman biked backwards through the pasture as easily as if we'd been coasting on pavement. He didn't stop until we reached Coolidge Castle.

People who stumble across this old mansion think it's deserted. Or haunted. Bart Coolidge lets weeds grow till they bend over and dry out. Only a strip of lawn in front of the house gets mowed to make room for plastic lawn ornaments. Today big orange balls lay on the stubby grass, probably the beginnings of Halloween decorations, even though Halloween was over a month away.

I slid off the bike, brushed off my jeans and shirt, and stared up at the three-story mansion that could have used a coat of paint. Several windows had boards hammered across them. Cats swarmed at my feet, but I didn't bend down to pet them.

Catman helped me up the creaky steps and inside. The cool, dark living room covered me with its perfume. The difference between the outside and inside of Coolidge Castle never failed to surprise me. Nothing inside the house was run-down, although most things were old. I could imagine stepping out of a time machine into a place a century or two ago. A giant chandelier cast a glow on velvet furniture, while thick red drapes kept sunlight out of a living room as big as our whole house.

Catman's mom descended the winding staircase in a lime green dress that reached to her matching fuzzy slippers. Her hair was totally wrapped in aluminum foil, probably some new hair treatment. "Calvin—ahhh! What happened to Winnie?"

"I'm okay." I braced myself as she scurried down the stairs and shuffled toward us. "Really. Just a sore shoulder—"

"Your hair!" Ignoring my black eye, Mrs. Coolidge dashed straight for my hair and began pulling out twigs and leaves. "What did you do to this gorgeous hair?"

I tried not to flinch as she combed her fingers through my hair. "Mrs. Coolidge?" At least my voice had come back, no hoarser than usual. "It's really all right."

"Calvin!" she scolded. "How could you let this happen? Get my hairbrush!"

Catman cleared his throat. "Mom." He called his parents Mom and Dad to their faces, but Claire and Bart otherwise. They always called him Calvin. "Check Winnie out—like, not just her hair."

For the first time, his mom looked directly at me. Her green eyes through her glasses grew as big as spit curls. "You have bruises around your eye!"

I shrugged, which made me wince.

"Check her shoulder," Catman said.

"What happened?" Mrs. Coolidge asked, poking my ribs.

"I fell." I got it out before Catman had a chance to answer.

Mrs. Coolidge dragged in a kitchen stool and made me sit. "Let's have a look at our shoulder."

She kneaded my arm as if I were bread dough. "No swelling. Nothing broken."

I nodded at Catman. "Told you!"

While Mrs. Coolidge jabbed me, waves of multicolored fur flowed at my feet, cats of all colors and sizes. Moggie, a small light-orange tabby, and Wilhemina scratched at the stool legs.

"Ow!" I cried when Mrs. Coolidge punched my shoulder.

"Sorry, dear. Our shoulder is not dislocated. But we have a nasty bruise there. That must have been quite a fall! Where did you—?"

"Mom?" Catman jerked his head toward the kitchen. "Do I smell brownies?"

"First things first, Calvin." She held out her palm, the surgeon waiting for her scalpel. "Brush!"

After Mrs. Coolidge performed hair surgery on me, she brought out chocolate milk with ice cubes and straws as long and winding as the Mississippi. Catman and I ate brownies the size of North and South Carolina.

I forced down food so they wouldn't think I was sick. But all I felt like doing was going home and curling up in my own bed. "Catman, will you tell Pat I'll answer my horse e-mails tomorrow after church?"

"That's cool."

I thanked Mrs. Coolidge. Catman trailed me to the door. I reached for the doorknob, and the door burst open.

Bart Coolidge entered like a gust of wind. He looks like a used-car salesman—maybe because he *is* a used-car salesman, owner of Smart Bart's Used Cars. His hairpiece lay crooked on his round head, and his Looney Tunes Taz tie was flipped back over his shoulder.

"Sa-a-ay!" he shouted. "Winnie! Listen to this one. So this fellow loses control of his automobile and crashes into a cornfield. He manages to drive the car into town, cornstalks sticking out his bumper. A boy observes said car as the fellow motors down Main Street. What do you think the lad asks his mother?"

I laughed. I may not always understand Bart Coolidge's jokes—and he does have a million of them. But he always makes me laugh, usually way before the punch line. "I give. What'd he say?"

"'Mommy, look at that bumper crop!' Get it? Bumper? Crop? I got a million of 'em!" He leaned in. "Young lady, have you and Calvin been fighting?"

I couldn't even imagine peace-loving Catman in a fight. "I fell."

"Bart!" yelled his wife from across the room.

"Claire!" They ran into each other's arms, like in a sappy, romantic movie.

Outside, Catman walked with me as far as the orange pumpkin-wanna-be balls. "I can ride you home," he offered.

"No thanks. I'm fine." I did feel better . . . on the outside. Inside I felt like a pinball machine, thoughts banking off each other and never scoring. What had really happened at that hedge?

A window opened, and Bart Coolidge yelled down, "What did the car say to the Canadian goose?"

I gave up, palms raised.

"Honk, eh?" He laughed in wind-filled huffs, like a donkey braying.

As I walked home, I replayed the jump in my mind. I'd been so sure I could get Beauty over that hedge.

At the pasture Nickers trotted up to meet me. She stuck her head over the fence, and I pressed my forehead against her silky cheek.

As I walked on to the house, I glanced back

at the hedge. It couldn't have grown in the last hour, but it seemed twice as tall as it had that afternoon.

Dad's truck, the old cattle truck we'd driven from Wyoming, hogged the curb in front of our house, so I knew he was home. I spotted him in the side yard. He was rocking frantically in his chair invention. I kept my head down and waved as I hurried inside.

Lizzy was clearing the table. "You missed dinner!"

"Not hungry." I darted back to our room. But I wasn't quick enough for my sister.

"Winnie!" She raced past me and blocked our bedroom doorway. "What happened? Did you get in a fight? I'll bet it was Summer Spidell! But you could beat her with your hands tied in a bow behind your back! Not that you *should* beat her! I didn't mean *that!* She must have had help! That's so unfair! Does it hurt? You have to get hold of that temper of yours—!"

"Lizzy!" I finally got a word in. "I didn't fight!"

Lizzy's green eyes widened. "You didn't? But your eye—!"

"I fell." I ducked under her arm and slipped into our room. "You know how clumsy I am."

No lies here. Not really. I did fall. I am clumsy.

"Are you okay? What did Dad say?"

"Lizzy, all I need is a good night's sleep." I kicked clothes out of the way, clearing a path to my unmade bed. Lizzy's bed was made with hospital corners, neat as her half of the room. "Don't make a big deal out of this to Dad. Tell him I'm fine. I fell. I'm going to bed."

I knew Lizzy wanted to ask a hundred questions. But I convinced her to go so I could rest.

When I was sure the coast was clear, I moved to the foot of my bed and gazed out the window, where night was taking over. Crickets chirped, growing soft, then loud, as if reading the same music. I could make out Nickers and Towaco grazing on either side of Bold Beauty as if they knew she needed a friend. *I'd* sure let her down.

In the middle of the night, I jerked bolt upright in bed, gasping for breath. My clothes stuck to me in a clammy sweat.

I'd had nightmares, replays of Bold Beauty in the air, the sound of the hedge scraping her belly. The landing. The fall. Catman's blurry face as I tried to breathe.

This is stupid! I've fallen before. It's just a nightmare, I told myself.

But it wasn't. The pictures were more real with my eyes open. Details formed, things I hadn't noticed—a glimpse of a white hoof boot, the reins slipping from my hands, a patch of clover as I thudded to the ground.

Over and over the pictures raced through my mind. Again and again, I fell. I couldn't stop the pictures. The nightmare wouldn't end.

Sunday I woke a dozen times before finally hauling myself out of bed. Nothing hurt except my shoulder. All I wanted was to get through the day without having anybody suspect I'd fallen off Bold Beauty.

When I looked in the mirror, I winced. A purple-green-yellow splotch circled my left eye. A matching bruise stretched from my left shoulder to my elbow.

Voices floated in from the kitchen, along with the scent of bacon and pancakes. Lizzy and Dad were laughing at something as I slipped into the bathroom. I hung a washcloth over the doorknob, our substitute for a lock, and ran the bathwater as hot as I could stand it.

After my bath, I braided my wet hair and

dressed in the same denim jumper I'd worn last Sunday, adding a long-sleeved shirt under it to hide my shoulder bruise. But there was nothing I could do for the bruise circling my eye.

Here we go, God, I prayed as I plastered on a smile and walked to the kitchen. "Morning, Lizzy! Dad!"

I made a beeline to the fridge and squatted behind the open door, conducting a slow search for the orange juice that sat on the top shelf.

"Heard you had a great fall, Humpty Dumpty," Dad said. "Must run in the family. First time I held your mother in my arms was when she tripped over a sidewalk crack and I caught her."

Even Lizzy didn't say anything. I could count on one hand the times Dad had said "your mother" over the past two years. I knew Dad thought about Mom as much as I did. But neither of us could bring ourselves to talk about her.

Things were changing, getting better. How could I wreck everything by telling Dad about my fall? What if he asked me to quit? We'd be back to fighting.

"What are you doing in that fridge?" Lizzy asked.

"Looking for juice."

"I already poured yours."

"Thanks." I didn't budge. Dad still hadn't seen my black eye. On the bottom shelf, I spotted the plastic bagful of rubber bands. "Um, Dad, why do you keep rubber bands in the fridge?"

"Haven't I explained the physics of that to you?" Dad put down his paper.

Bingo! I'd hooked him.

"Rubber bands last longer when kept cold," Dad explained. "It's a question of contraction and elasticity and—"

I closed the fridge and made a break for the table.

". . . chemical reaction with the particles— Winnie!" Dad shouted. "Your eye!"

"Looks worse than it is, Dad." I slapped two pancakes on my plate, poured syrup over them, and dug in. Couldn't talk with my mouth full.

"But how . . . ?" Dad leaned in for a better look.

"Yeah!" Lizzy pulled up a chair. "I thought about that all night. I mean, did you fall in the street? Was Catman with you? What are you going to do about your eye when you go to school and—"

While Lizzy rattled on, I kept chewing on my pancake, holding up one finger, the sorry-I-can't-talk-my-mouth's-full sign.

Finally, I swallowed. "Lizzy, great pancakes! What flavor is this?" My sister loves cooking almost as much as Dad loves inventing.

"Bubblegum!" Lizzy exclaimed. "Do you like it? Mix vanilla, cinnamon, and wintergreen, and you get bubblegum flavor!"

Dad coughed and set down his fork. "I was trying to place that taste."

I felt like I should keep chewing, even though I'd swallowed everything.

Dad glanced at the clock. "When are the Barkers picking up you girls for church?"

"About an hour," Lizzy answered.

"I think I'll come along."

"That's so tight, Dad!" Lizzy exclaimed.

I agreed. "That's great!"

In Wyoming the four of us had gone to church every Sunday. No discussion. But Dad hadn't been to church since Mom's funeral. I knew he hadn't stopped believing in God. But Mom had kind of taken the family lead in the God department. And after Mom died, Lizzy was the one who kept us praying before meals.

I hoped Dad liked the Ashland church.

Dad left, and Lizzy scooted closer, chin in hands. "Okay, Winnie. What's up? Why didn't you go riding this morning? You ride every Sunday morning before church—unless it's raining hard or maybe too icy. Are you hurt or what?"

"Can't I sleep in for once?" I forced myself to take another bite of bubblegum pancake. To tell the truth, I didn't know why I hadn't ridden.

Lizzy wouldn't let it go. "But you never—"

"Lizzy, how's that spider of yours doing?" I asked, changing the subject.

Lizzy sat back, arms crossed, and raised her eyebrows at me so I'd know *she* knew I was trying to change the subject. But she couldn't help herself. I was inviting her to talk about her beloved spiders. "He ate his own web, Winnie! The whole thing! I watched. Then he spit it out and designed a whole new web! This one's even better than the last one! You ought to see it."

I stood up. "Good idea. I'll go look right now."

I made my escape and stayed outside with the horses until almost time to go.

Dad stepped out of the house as I walked up.

He had on the suit he'd worn at Mom's funeral. He must have lost weight because it hung on him. Dad used to wear a different suit every day to his office. But he'd left them along the way, in the *I* states, replacing dress suits with one-piece work suits.

I sat on the front step next to Dad.

"Your mother would have liked this, Winnie."

Your mother. Twice in the same morning. I knew what Dad meant. Mom would have liked all of us going to church again.

A fall breeze rustled the leaves, making a shower of brown and gold in the sunlight. We didn't speak but sat there together, listening to morning birds. It felt good. I didn't want anything to spoil it.

"A lot of things have gone right lately, don't you think?" he asked.

I nodded.

Dad put his arm around me. "Except that shiner."

I tasted bubblegum pancakes that wanted to come up. I wanted to come clean, to tell him about Beauty, how I'd really gotten the bruises.

But I couldn't risk it. Our relationship was like

a delicate spiderweb. If I tugged out a thread,
I was afraid the whole web would be destroyed
and we'd have to start over from scratch.

*M*rs. Barker drove up in the Barker bus, a yellow van that looked more like a school bus. Johnny and Luke, Barker's four-year-old and six-year-old brothers, stuck their heads out of windows and yelled for Lizzy to sit by them. Great-granny Barker sat by the open front window, her white hair blown wild around her wrinkled face. If I had a great-granny, I'd want her to be like Granny Barker.

Mr. Barker climbed out of the backseat, where he'd been wedged between Mark, who was seven, and the youngest boy, William, who was two. He met my dad on the lawn. "Good to see you, Jack. Coming with us?"

Mr. Barker's not as tall as my dad, but his

neck is about twice as big around. He used to play football at Ashland University, where he now teaches poetry. Mrs. Barker teaches there, too. I was glad they didn't make Dad feel bad for not going to church before now.

"You look pretty full in there. I'll just take the truck." Dad made a move toward the cattle truck.

"Get in, Jack!" Mrs. Barker shouted. "We'll make room." She did a double take of me. "Winnie, girl! What happened to your eye?"

"Isn't it awful?" Lizzy exclaimed. "She fell!"

The boys hung out of windows and groaned. "Yuk!" "Gross!"

Lizzy squeezed in back with the boys. Dad and I took the middle seat with Matthew, the second oldest son at nine. He was the only Barker whose face didn't fall into a natural smile. His dog was a bulldog, and it suited him.

"Hey, Matthew!" I buckled in next to him. "How's Bull?"

Matthew frowned. "Mean and dangerous."

"Is not!" Luke screamed. He's six but small for his age, like his puppy, Chico.

"Is so!" Matthew yelled back.

I was kind of glad to see them argue. The Barkers are the happiest family I've ever been around. It was nice to know they weren't perfect.

Minutes later, Mrs. Barker pulled into the church lot and backed into a narrow parking place.

"Nice, isn't it, Dad?" The church was a lot smaller than ours in Wyoming, but I loved the way the maples hugged the white steeple. I hoped Dad would love it, too.

We walked to the front of the church and filed into the Barker pew, me last.

Pat Haven hollered at us from across the aisle.

Dad waved, but I slouched, hiding my eye with the hymnal.

Organ music started, and Catman strolled down the aisle as if he'd waited for it. He wore white sandals, light blue bell-bottoms, and a high-necked, wide-sleeved shirt that could have come from a Hollywood wardrobe room. He scooted in next to me.

Dad leaned across me. "Nice Nehru shirt, Catman! I used to have one just like it!"

Catman gave Dad the peace sign.

We stood and sang the first hymn. Then

Ralph Evans, the substitute pastor, strolled to the front of the church and motioned us to sit. In khakis and tennis shoes, Ralph didn't look much like a pastor. His real job was running the animal shelter. The old pastor had moved on to a bigger church in Akron. Barker said Ralph had agreed to fill in until the church could make up its mind on a new pastor.

I started to explain Ralph to Dad, but I was too late.

"Mornin'!" Ralph shouted. "Anybody here for the first time?"

Note to self: If I'm ever a substitute pastor, don't make first-timers raise their hands! I felt so uncomfortable for Dad.

Dad raised his hand.

I looked around. One woman, about a hundred years old, raised her hand, too. I thought I'd seen her in church before.

"Well, welcome!" Ralph grinned at Dad. "I'm just filling in as pastor. Some of you may have met me down at the animal shelter. I admit I'm not much of a speaker. But that's all right, I guess. This way if I say anything that makes sense, we can be pretty sure it comes from the good Lord."

People chuckled. I glanced at Dad but

couldn't tell if he was smiling or gritting his teeth.

Ralph prayed with his eyes open. "God, thanks for this pretty day! I couldn't have thought up all these colors if you gave me all eternity to do it!" Then he went on, thanking God for stuff, including "the new people."

Finally, he got to his sermon. "I like the name *Jesus*. But I also love the name we hear around Christmas—*Immanuel*. It means 'God with us.' Isn't that a great thing! I know. We're still in September. But Immanuel isn't just for Christmas. He's for every day of the year. After all, it's only when I forget that God's always 'with us' that I end up in a mess of trouble. But when I remember Jesus is with me, things work out."

Ralph read the story about the disciples getting caught in a fishing boat during a raging storm. "Can't you just see those big, brave fishermen scared silly? And Jesus sleeping in the back of the boat, calm as you please? I bet those fishermen tried every skill they had until one of 'em remembered Jesus was on board! Immanuel. And that's all it took to get them out of that mess."

When church ended, I wanted to hurry out to the van before Pat spotted me. No such luck.

"Whoa! Winnie!" Pat blocked the aisle. "Any-who, how's it going?"

Could she have missed my black eye? "Fine. Thanks."

"Swell!" Pat greeted my dad, then turned back to me. "I can give you a lift to the pet store if you want to answer those horse e-mails now."

I glanced at Dad. "I probably should catch up on the Pet Help Line."

"Good idea," Dad said.

I followed Pat to her car. She swept up her red-and-white checked dress to get in and then flung her straw church hat into the backseat.

We were out of the church lot when she asked, "So, Winnie, how did you get your shiner?"

A setup! Winnie Willis, you should have seen it coming! I stared out the window, imagining a getaway on Nickers. "I fell."

"Uh-huh," Pat mumbled.

I faked a laugh. "Clumsy as an ox—no offense!"

She didn't laugh at my imitation of her "no offense" line. Pat was tougher than Lizzy and

Dad put together. "What did you do after I left yesterday?"

"Hung out with Catman." I willed her to drive faster.

"Didn't jump that hunter, did you?" she asked.

"Beauty's going to make an ace jumper, Pat!" I was doing word gymnastics to keep from out-and-out lying. "And thanks to your help, she's not scared of cars anymore."

"Mmm-hmm."

I could have walked faster than Pat drove.

"So everything went fine with Beauty?"

"Sure." Okay, not fine exactly. It was getting tougher to dance around the truth.

"Anything else you want to tell me, Winnie?"

"Just that I'm sorry about being too chicken to debate abortion."

When Pat didn't jump in with her "no offense" line, I cleared my throat. "Did you get anybody else yet?"

"Huh-uh."

Finally we pulled up in front of Pat's Pets, a brick building off Main Street. Pat unlocked the door. When she turned on the lights, dogs barked and birds fluttered against their cages.

Woooo-hoo! The wolf whistle could only belong to Hawk's chattering lory. Peter zoomed at us and landed on Pat's shoulder.

"Peter! You fresh thing!" Pat scolded.

I petted his bright red head the way Hawk did. "You miss Hawk, Peter?"

Peter bobbed his head. *"Ring! Ring! Who's there?"*

"Just Winnie," I answered. "And I'd better get to those e-mails."

"I'll be upstairs if you need me." Pat headed for the steps at the far end of the store.

Pat and her husband used to live in our house, the one we rent from her now. When he died, Pat opened the pet shop and moved into the attic apartment.

Pat called down from the top of the stairs, "Peter, here, would sure like to know how you really got hurt."

I tried to laugh. "Tell Peter curiosity killed the cat. No offense."

Pat didn't laugh. I heard her door shut.

Sorry, God, I prayed as I waited for the computer to boot up. *As soon as I figure out what went wrong at that hedge, I'll tell Pat . . . and Dad and Lizzy . . . everything.*

Another picture of the fall flashed into my brain. I fought it off.

Logging onto the help line, I checked out the homepage Barker was working on for the Pet Help Line. The moving graphics looked great but took a long time to load.

Pat padded downstairs again, and I prepared to be interrogated. Instead she handed me a plastic grocery bag. "Thought you might need these for school until that bruise heals."

I peered into the bagful of makeup stuff. "Thanks, Pat."

"And whatever you really did to get that thing, don't do it again." Pat walked off, Peter Lory still on her shoulder, pecking at her brown curls.

Feeling guiltier than ever, I opened the in-box and scrolled through all the e-mails since Friday. One of Barker's made me think of Chico.

> My Schnauzer, Muffin, won't stop barking when we go on our walk! I love my fluffy, wuffy baby Muffy Wuffy. I pick her up and tell her, "Mama's baby shouldn't barky warky." But she simply

will not listen to her mommy! What's a
mommy to do????
—Princess

Barker had answered:

Dear Princess,
   Dogs usually bark because they're
afraid. If you pick Muffin up when she
sees another dog, she'll really think
she's in danger. She'll believe you've
picked her up to keep her safe. My
advice is to let her walk. And one more
tip: some dogs understand 2,000
words—but no baby talk. They like
clear cues. Hope this helps!
—Barker

My favorite Catman e-mail was actually about
jumping, kind of:

Catman!
   My cat won't stop jumping onto the
kitchen counter. I think it's really cute.
But Mom says if I can't get Claribel 2
stop jumping on her counter, she's
going 2 give Claribel away! If she does,

I'm running away. U have any other
ideas?
—Katz

Cool it, Katz!
   Don't leave your digs yet, man.
Plan A: Spread syrup over the counter.
Cats hate sticky feet. Claribel will get
the picture and steer clear. Plan B: In
case Mrs. Katz isn't cool with the syrup
gig, cover the whole counter with
aluminum foil. Claribel will freak out
at the noise and hate that counter. So
be cool, Katz!
—The Catman

Twelve horse e-mails waited for me. Eight
of them got the same solution, even though
the problems ranged from stall-kicking to friski-
ness. The horses needed more turnout time,
more freedom to run and play. Otherwise that
energy comes out in a way that makes owners
write to me about their "problem horses." Most
of the time it's the people who are the problems.
   I took my time answering the other e-mails.

Dear Winnie,

Help! My horse, Shirley, won't stop eating! Every time I go on a trail ride with my friends, I get laughed @. Shirley stops and grazes, and I can't get her head back up. Shirley is huge, and I'm not. It's not fair! How can I get her 2 quit trying 2 eat grass when I'm riding her?

—Embarrassed!

I could picture Embarrassed tugging as hard as she could on the reins, with old Shirley munching away.

Embarrassed,

When Shirley does graze, you might as well admit you can't outpull her to raise her head. Don't try! You might lose and get yourself pulled over her head! Instead, squeeze your knees into her sides and urge her forward. She'll have to raise her head whether she likes it or not. Bad habits are hard to break. Better start by washing that bit so Shirley won't be tempted by the taste of grass. Then try to read her actions and urge her on faster before she lowers her head to graze. And remember, she's just doing what comes naturally to a horse. Don't be too hard on her.

—Winnie

At the end of my messages, there was one from Hawk—all the way from Paris. I couldn't wait to open it. I'd first gotten to know Hawk through e-mails on the Pet Help Line. Seeing her name pop up in my in-box reminded me of our e-mail friendship, which had been a lot easier than our face-to-face friendship. I clicked on her message.

Hello, Winnie,

We made it! Tomorrow we visit L'Ecole Internationale. Call me a Birdbrain if you like (I do consider it a compliment), but I still have not told my parents I don't want to go to boarding school. I wish I had half your confidence.

I miss Peter! I left my other birds with our neighbor, but—

The message stopped in midsentence, then picked up a few lines down:

> URGENT! URGENT! URGENT!
>
> I hope you are reading this! My "New Mail" just beeped. It was Summer Spidell! She says Richard has found a new horse for the Howards! And he's talked to somebody about buying Howard's Lionhearted Lady as a camp horse. What's going on, Winnie? What happened to Bold Beauty?

$\mathcal{I}$ could hardly sleep Sunday night. I kept imagining Bold Beauty trudging through the same boring routine, ridden by camp kids who didn't appreciate her. She was a born hunter. She'd never be happy walking in circles all day long.

More than ever, I determined not to let anyone know Beauty had thrown me on the high jump. If Summer found out, she'd tell the Howards, and that would be the end of my chance with Beauty. I'd cover up my black eye and do everything I could to stay away from Summer—no big sacrifice there.

Monday morning I spent 30 minutes in the bathroom experimenting with Pat's makeup.

When I finally joined Lizzy in the kitchen, I knew my attempt at glamour had failed.

Lizzy's face crinkled. "Winnie? What's the matter with your face?"

My sister spent another 30 minutes on me. "Isn't this fun!" she exclaimed, dabbing something on my cheeks.

"Ow!" I flinched when she pressed too hard under my left eye.

"Sorry! Anything for beauty, right? Well, of course, not really. Beauty's on the inside, which is a good thing because all the makeup in the world won't hide this purple-and-yellow blotch under your eye, Winnie. God, please help Winnie's shiner heal super fast."

Lizzy prayed like our mom, slipping back and forth so smoothly between heaven and earth conversations it was hard to keep them straight.

I faced the mirror and wondered if Mom would have approved of me wearing makeup to school. It didn't look half bad until I got close up. My black eye shone through, plain as night.

Dad was already hard at work on his rocking chair when I hopped on my back bike and headed for Ashland Middle School. He didn't even comment on the new, made-up Winnie.

I didn't mind. I felt lucky to make a clean getaway.

At AMS, I shoved my bike into the rack and tried to push through the herd of kids on the steps. Sometimes I picture cliques and groups of students as herds of horses, like the Mustangs Mom and I had observed in the wilderness. Herds don't like to let newcomers into the group. Horses try to impress each other. They struggle to be the leader. Only difference between horses and people is that horses are easier to talk to.

I kept my head down and saw more brands of tennis shoes than there are breeds of horses.

Keep a low profile. Nobody will notice.

"Winnie?"

I recognized Grant Baines's voice. He and I ran in different *herds* at school. But I'd helped train Grant's Quarter Horse and discovered he wasn't too bad . . . for a popular kid.

"Winnie! Come over!" Grant shouted so loud that half the kids on the steps turned around. So much for a low profile!

I trudged over, my nose buried in my math book for the first time all year. "Hi, Grant," I muttered.

Summer, Salena, and two other seventh-graders circled Grant like moons around a planet. Grant's a head taller than me, and has thick brown hair and dimples that make girls act silly around him. Salena was one of Summer's friends. I think she's a redhead, but it's hard to tell because she tries out so many colors. Today her red hair had a green streak on one side.

"I hear we're both on the next life science debate," Grant said.

I shook my head. "Not me."

Salena, a.k.a. Sal, jumped in. "I thought Barker said you were! I finally volunteered. No way I want in on the next debate, that animal rights one. Like I could choose between giving up cosmetics or saving fuzzy guinea pigs! You sure you're not on a debate team?"

I shook my head again. *Witty conversation, Winnie. Amazing you're not on the debate team with verbal skills like this!*

Grant cocked his head. "You look different today."

"You're wearing makeup!" Sal exclaimed. Sal wore makeup every day, lots of it, with fake eyelashes and glitter eye shadow.

I stared at my toes.

Sal's even taller than Grant and so thin not an ounce of flab showed when her short T-shirt rose higher than her low-cut khakis. "Kind of looks tight. Love that shade of blush!" Then, like a giraffe checking out lower branches, she bent down for a better look. "But something's weird. . . . You have a black eye, Winnie!"

Great. Could you say it louder?

Grant laughed. "Get in a fight?"

Funny how everyone figured hotheaded Winnie had been in a fight. At least it kept them from suspecting the truth.

Summer, who had stared off into space since I joined their little clique, came to life. "A black eye?"

I retied my shoelaces. "I . . . ran into a door."

Why did I say that? Saying I fell may not have been the *whole* truth, but it wasn't a real lie.

I faked a laugh. "Gotta get to my locker. Later." As I hurried away from them, I felt Summer's cold glare on my back. The hairs on my neck tingled.

Okay, God. That one was an all-out lie. I'm so sorry. It just came out. But I knew better. The door explanation sounded more believable than a fall. And even saying "fall" in front of Summer could be dangerous.

But it felt crummy to be a liar. A black-eyed liar.

I hustled to English class and slid into my seat next to Barker.

"Your eye looks better," Barker whispered.

Count on Eddy Barker to say the right thing. For the first time, it struck me that Barker was getting to look more like his dad—more muscles, taller. Even his black, curly hair had been cut short like Mr. Barker's.

"Class?" Ms. Brumby stood in front of her desk. If our English teacher were a horse, she'd be a cross between a Barb and a Brumby, which is pretty funny since that's her name—Barb Brumby. She has the frizzed hair and Roman nose of the Australian scrub horse, the Brumby. And she's as tough as the North African Barb.

But she dresses better, with suits in more colors than horses' hide and matching shoes. Today, total orangeness. Just once I'd like to see her grab the wrong shoes and show up in a green dress and blue shoes. She couldn't handle it.

"Our next debate will have to be on a Saturday this time. We want all parents to have an opportunity to attend. Saturday evening is the soonest we can get use of the school gymnasium."

Great. Now I *knew* I wouldn't volunteer. At least the other debates had been right after school, when most of the parents couldn't even show up.

"We have four volunteers for the side I'm coaching, pro-choice. But Barker and Sal still need two more volunteers for their pro-life team."

Sal? I figured she'd be on the other team.

Note to self: Don't jump to conclusions.

"Any volunteers?" Ms. Brumby asked.

My heart pounded. *Please, somebody!*

Ms. Brumby frowned.

Barker glanced at me, then back to Ms. Brumby. "I'm sure we'll get more in life science," he said.

"I hope so." Ms. Brumby moved to the blackboard and started writing our assignments.

I wanted to go home and scream into a pillow. Not only was I a liar, I was a coward.

By the time I got to life science, a dozen kids had asked about my eye. I'd stuck with the door explanation, which got easier and easier to give.

Pat Haven rushed into class, dropped a stack of papers on the desk, and caught her breath. "We got ourselves a problem! I still need two more volunteers for our next debate. We have to get moving on this, folks."

It had been bad enough wimping out in Brumby's class. Letting Pat Haven down was going to be torture.

Nobody volunteered.

Summer muffled a laugh. I wheeled around to glare at her. She was whispering to Grant. I wanted to pull her out of her chair by her golden curls.

"Anybody?" Pat asked. "Don't forget. You'll have to be on a debate team sooner or later."

Still no takers.

Most of the kids didn't seem to mind talking in front of people. Why weren't *they* volunteering? I'd kept putting off debating because I wouldn't be any good at it. I can talk a horse into almost anything. But people? No way.

"Might as well give up, Mrs. Haven." Summer sounded bored. "Nobody else is going to argue against a woman's right to choose."

"You may be right, Summer," Pat admitted. "But I sure hope not."

"This is a stupid debate anyway," Summer muttered, loud enough for us to hear. "Haven ought to get with the times. Abortion's been legal for years."

Something inside me snapped. "It—that doesn't mean right!" It hadn't come out like I'd wanted it to.

"What?" Summer smirked and glanced at Sal for backup.

Barker took over. "Winnie said that just because abortion was legalized, that doesn't mean it's right."

"That's not what Winnie said." Summer laughed and stared right at me. "What *did* you say, Winnie?" She said it like she was talking to a four-year-old.

I didn't trust myself to answer.

"Maybe you're saving it for the debate," Summer suggested. "Oooh—I hope we don't all end up with black eyes!"

My stomach tied in knots, like my tongue.

"There aren't enough on your side to have the debate, Mrs. Haven!" Brian shouted. "So . . . we win!"

"You do not!" I shouted back. My ears roared and my face burned.

"Are *you* volunteering?" Summer asked.

"Yeah!" I blurted out. It was like hearing someone else say it. Not me. Certainly not me.

"Hot dog!" Pat exclaimed. "No offense. Three down, one to go!"

"You said it could be *any* seventh-grader, right? If we didn't get enough from the class? Catman will recruit somebody!" Barker promised, patting my bruised shoulder. I didn't feel it. I was too numb.

I didn't look at Summer, but I heard her whisper to Sal, "This should be good. I can hardly wait to see Winnie in action!"

Mom always warned me that my temper would get me into trouble my whole life if I didn't get a handle on it. Now I'd really done it. As if I didn't have enough to worry about with Bold Beauty, I, Winnie the Tongue-Tied Horse Gentler, was now on a debate team!

𝔦 caught up with Catman in the cafeteria and
waited until he sat across from me, his tray
loaded with everything the cafeteria ladies had
to offer. Between worrying about the debate
and Beauty's high jump, my stomach was too
knotted to eat. "Catman, you haven't talked to
any seventh-graders about joining Barker's
debate team, have you?"

He scarfed the top of his hamburger bun in
two bites and shook his head.

"Don't try too hard," I pleaded. "Or better yet,
find *two* people! I sort of accidentally said I'd be
on Barker's team, but—"

"Cool." He inhaled the bottom bun, then
started on the burger.

"No! *Not* cool! I'd make a fool of myself,

Catman. Plus, I'd make the pro-life side look stupid!"

Catman squinted at my eye and handed me his napkin.

I dabbed at the makeup.

"Heard you ran into a door." Catman didn't look up from the peas he scooped onto his knife.

My lie sounded even lamer coming from Catman. I couldn't think of anything to say.

Catman rejoined the food line for seconds.

All around kids shouted, making plans for after school. Silverware banged. Trays clattered.

I glanced at Summer and Grant's table and thought about Hawk's e-mail. Maybe Summer had made it up about finding a horse to replace Beauty. I wouldn't have put it past her. A tray plunked down across from me.

"Catman—," I started.

But it wasn't Catman. I recognized the kid from my English class who sat in the back and hadn't said one word since school started. His hair, pulled back in a ponytail, was longer than Catman's, but black, like everything he wore every single day. Even in August, he'd shown up in black jeans and a black turtleneck.

I started to warn him he was in Catman's spot, but thought better of it. Catman could take care of himself. Instead, I tried to smile. "Hi . . ." I didn't even know his name.

He glanced at me, then went back to his burger.

"How's it going?" I tried again.

This time he didn't even look up.

Fine. I'd wait until Catman got back. Nobody takes the Catman's seat.

Catman walked up and, without a pause, slid in next to the kid in black. They might have been in a french-fry race, matching each other as they ate fry for fry in silence. When Catman had finished every bite of his seconds, he said, "M, this is Winnie."

So *this* was M! I'd heard M stories ever since we'd moved to Ashland. Kids joked about what the *M* stood for—Mystery, Moody, Maniac, Mute.

"We're in Brumby's class together," I said. "So what's the *M* stand for?"

M shot me a look as if I'd asked him why his mother wore army boots.

Catman shoved his tray away. "Done." Compared to M, he was downright talkative.

At least I didn't have to worry about M blab-bing. "Catman, I'm riding Beauty as soon as I'm done with the Pet Help Line. I have to get her to take that high jump."

He raised his eyebrows.

"Don't say that!" I protested. "I can do this in my sleep."

Catman locked his bright blues on me. "No doorknobs this time?"

"Look, I'm going to tell everybody the truth . . . eventually. I just need to make the jump first. Okay? I'm sure I can do it this time."

Luckily Pat had a lot of customers at Pat's Pets after school, so she didn't get a chance to quiz me. Barker settled in a new litter of puppies while I watched Catman answer his last e-mail at lightning speed, using only his thumbs and pinkies.

> Catman,
>   A pilot friend claims you solved his cat problem after three cat psycholo-gists failed. We're flight attendants and

have a Siamese cat in our Chicago apartment. When we're gone, Cuddles takes her revenge and scratches my favorite couch—never anything else. Any advice?
—Cat-loving Stewardesses

Catman didn't even pause to think of his answer:

Peace, Stewardesses!
You can stop that scratching by chowing down an orange. Pin the orange peel to that couch. Cats hate the smell of oranges. Cuddles won't hang there again. But hey, man! You should rap about getting another cat. Cuddles is lonely! Thanks for writing— gives me a chance to practice left-handed typing. *Stewardesses* is the longest English word you can type with the left hand. Fly high!
—Catman

Catman walked off to find Peter Lory, and I took over. Right away I spotted a message from Hawk and saved it until I'd finished the help-line e-mails. Sunday I'd lied to Hawk, too, and promised that Beauty and I were fine. Maybe this time, on e-mail, I could tell her the truth.

It didn't take long to answer five horse e-mails. Then I scrolled down to Hawk's:

> Winnie!
> Great news about Bold Beauty! I should have known Winnie the Horse Gentler wouldn't fail when it came to horses!
> Guess what I saw in the grasslands! My first golden plover! It had long legs, like the Ohio plover, the one Lizzy calls "killdeer." When I got close to the nest, the bird spread out her wings and pretended to be hurt. She led me away from her babies and faked injury to protect them.
> Mother is calling. No, I have not gotten the courage to tell her yet.
> —Hawk

How could I tell Hawk about my problem when she had her own? I dashed off a quick pep talk to encourage her to talk to her parents. I ended with "You can do it! So just do it!"

At home, all three horses came into the barn

to greet me. It felt great to be around horses after a day of dealing with humans. If there was any place in the world I had confidence, this was it. Nothing was stopping me from taking that high jump.

Except that the stalls needed cleaning. After mucking them, I grained the horses, measuring out the special oat mix I keep in plastic bins. Beauty finished her oats and came back for more. She snorted gently and nuzzled me. I slipped my arms around her neck and smelled the warmth. Chilly nights had brought on horse fuzz, the first stage of her winter coat.

"You deserve a good owner like Adrianna," I murmured.

I was halfway to the tack box to get the jumping saddle when I changed my mind. No sense making Nickers jealous by jumping Beauty. I really should ride my own horse first.

Nickers stood still while I slipped on the hackamore, her bitless bridle, and swung up bareback. She quivered, ready to go. I hugged her neck, feeling safe.

We rode away from the barn, far away from the hedge that loomed in the pasture. I turned down an overgrown lane blanketed with brown leaves. A flock of birds took off in a fury of wings.

Can we just stay here forever, God?

The lane grew narrower, then disappeared into weeds. I let Nickers choose her own path and her own pace. She must have read my heart. Nickering softly, my Arabian moved through the field, surefooted and controlled. When we came to a fence, she turned around.

As we neared the barn, Nickers pranced. She may have been eager to see Towaco and Beauty. Or she might have sensed my anxiety.

I cooled Nickers down. Then instead of saddling Beauty, I hopped on Hawk's good-natured Appaloosa. Towaco had worked his way out of every vice he'd picked up at Stable-Mart. Anybody could ride him now.

After a quick ride on the Appy, I trotted back to the paddock, where Lizzy and Catman were waiting.

"Why aren't you riding the new horse?" Lizzy asked.

"I will." I dismounted, careful not to look at Catman.

"Catman told me you're on Barker's don't-have-abortions debate team! That so rocks,

Winnie!" Lizzy hopped off the fence. "Can you hold off on riding the jumping horse until after dinner?"

"Sure!" I must have sounded too eager. Catman shook his head. Quickly I added, "I'll work Beauty after dinner."

But even as I said the words, pictures flooded my head—the hedge below me, Beauty's neck as I fell, Catman's shadowy face as I lay flat on my back.

We found Dad rocking in his chair like a crazy man. Sweat dripped off his forehead, although it was sweatshirt weather.

Catman pulled a rolled-up paper from his pocket and handed it to Dad.

Dad stopped rocking. He took the paper, then handed it back. "Catman, I told you I'm not ready. What if I won, not that I ever would? What would I do with Winnie and Lizzy while I'm at some Invention Convention?"

"You didn't enter that Inventor's Contest yet?" Lizzy squealed.

Catman handed back the paper. "Claire and Bart said our pad is your pad. You win, we'll keep the girls."

Lizzy and I exchanged looks of terror.

Coolidge Castle? Talk about your nice place to visit . . . but you wouldn't want to live there.

But Dad wasn't biting anyway. For some reason, he didn't seem to want to enter that contest.

Just as well.

Dad tossed the application down and revved up his rocker. "See? It's just not working." He rocked faster and pointed to the fan blades on top of the wind pole. "Stick your hands up there."

We did. A trickle of wind came out. Nothing compared to Dad's huffs and puffs.

He stopped. "Some invention."

We ate a quick meal of corn fish—Lizzy's variation on corn dogs, using fish sticks instead of hot dogs. Then Dad returned to his invention, and I headed back to the barn.

I decided to work Beauty on the lunge line, letting her jump riderless on the end of the long, nylon line.

I set out the five poles, or cavalletti, in a grid, spacing them along the ground so Beauty could canter over them without shifting her stride.

Next I laid out a series of low jumps, raising the poles nine inches off the ground, adding in two medium fence jumps, and letting the hedge serve as the final high jump.

Beauty cantered easily at the end of the lunge, flying over the ground poles and low jumps as if they weren't there. She loved to jump.

I kept her low-jumping on the lunge until dusk. Then I brought her in and cooled her off.

"How was your ride?" Dad asked when I walked up. He turned off the yard light.

"Great!" Half-truth. Beauty had done great. I hadn't even ridden.

Dad opened the door. "Coming?"

"In a minute." I gazed at the moon as Dad went inside. Clouded beams dabbed light around weird shadows in the yard.

I started for the door.

"Yuk!" Something sticky grabbed my arms. I brushed wildly, trying to get it off, knowing I'd walked smack-dab into a spiderweb. Imagining the spider pouncing on me and crawling all over my skin, I rubbed my arms and stamped my feet.

Lizzy's spider? I knew it couldn't have been Lizzy's pet, but I walked back to her spider tree to make sure. Moonlight struck the spider's

fancy web, outlining silvery lace patterns and
sparkling pearls.

In the corner of the web, Lizzy's spider waited
with his prizes—three lumps wrapped in silk,
insects hopelessly trapped.

Hopelessly trapped.

That's how I felt when I thought about jumping that hedge.

No! I can do it! I can. . . .

But it felt like a lie, a lie to myself.

My mind flashed to Beauty chasing Pat's car.
Pat had said something about giving Beauty a
false confidence. Was that what I'd had myself—
false confidence? Because somewhere inside me
a voice screamed that I could no more jump
that hedge than Beauty could chase a car.

I ran back to the house, still trying to get the
sticky cobweb off. But it followed me every
step. I couldn't get unstuck. I couldn't shake it
off.

$\mathcal{L}$ittle Miss Muffet was a real girl, you know."
My sister's voice floated in darkness above our
beds as the night outside grew darker.

I wished I'd never told her about my run-in
with the spiderweb. She hadn't stopped chattering about the creatures.

"Thomas Muffet was a spider expert," Lizzy
continued. "He made his daughter eat mashed
spiders when she got sick. People thought eating
spiders would cure a cold."

I pulled the covers over my head. "Night,
Lizzy! Please?"

But I couldn't sleep. Every time I dozed off,
pictures of the hedge crept into my brain, and
I'd jerk myself awake.

Tuesday in English, Ms. Brumby didn't say a word about the debate. And she didn't bring it up the next day or the next. Meanwhile, Pat Haven made a plea in her class every single day, so heartfelt I could have volunteered all over again.

But it was just as well I didn't have to worry about the debate. I had enough on my mind. All week I practiced Beauty over the pole jumps and parallels—always riderless. I kept reassuring myself that I had plenty of time to ride Beauty. The Howards weren't due back from their honeymoon until a week from Saturday.

But the more I told myself everything was fine, the more I doubted my own word. I knew better than anybody how many lies I'd handed out lately.

On Friday, I could tell by Pat's face that nobody had come through at the last minute and volunteered for her debate team. She begged the class one last time, then gave up and made us open our books to the chapter on senses.

"What do you kids know about the way animals see?" Pat sounded like the spunk had drained out of her.

"My cat's eyes glow in the dark," Kristine offered. I'd never spoken to Kristine. She had short blonde hair, dark eyebrows, and dark eyes. All I knew about her was that she seemed smart and she ran with Summer's crowd. "But it's actually reflected light not absorbed by the retina."

"Uh-huh." Pat glanced around the room. "Anybody else?"

Barker raised his hand. "Most dogs see great, but they're not big on colors."

"Uh-huh." Normally, Pat would have been bouncing around room, cheering for each answer, instead of slouching behind her desk.

Brian raised his hand. "Bats are blind as a bat—no offense!"

Half of the class laughed. I hated it. It felt like they were making fun of Pat. And she felt bad enough already.

I swallowed hard and raised my hand, something I don't usually do in class unless I need to go to the bathroom.

Pat sighed. "Winnie?"

I cleared my throat. "Horses' eyes are set on the sides so they can see almost all the way around, except for blind spots right in front and right behind."

My mind flashed that picture of me on Beauty heading for the hedge. How could she jump something so tall when she couldn't even see it in front of her? But that was silly. All horses have blind spots, not just Beauty. And if they have confidence in the rider, they're okay not seeing everything in front of them.

Pat was asking me something. ". . . anything else?"

"Um . . . horses see independently out of each eye, but that gives them poor depth vision. They may not know if something is a foot away or three feet away."

Did Beauty know how far she was from the hedge? Again, it wouldn't have mattered, not if she could have gotten confidence from me. Maybe I was the one who couldn't read how far we were from the hedge.

I didn't hear much of what other kids said about their pets. I kept trying to picture that hedge the instant before we jumped.

Kids began to shuffle their papers and grab their backpacks, signaling class was almost over.

Pat took a deep breath and gave it one more try. "Well, this is it, kiddos. Last chance before we have to move to the next topic. Any takers on the abortion debate?"

Summer sighed so loud she sounded like Catman's camel-moan tornado horn.

Nobody spoke up.

Barker silently begged, his colt eyes turned on each student.

"Then I guess," Pat said, "since today's the deadline, we'll change the topic to—"

Somebody knocked at the door.

We all turned to see Catman Coolidge, nose pressed to the windowpane high in the door.

Pat opened the door. "Catman?"

Without a word, he handed her a note and left.

Pat walked back to her desk, unfolding the note. "Yippee! The debate is on!"

"What happened?" Barker asked, already out of his seat.

"Catman came through! He's recruited a fourth member for the pro-life debate team."

"Who'd he get?" Brian hollered.

Pat squinted at the wrinkled paper.

"Well?" Summer demanded. "Who is it?"

"I'm not rightly sure," Pat said slowly. "I reckon this is just an initial. All it says is *M.*"

Kids were laughing hard as they poured out of Pat's classroom into the crowded hall.

I hung back with Barker. "Barker, what are we going to do? The debate is tomorrow. And M talks less than I do!"

Barker beamed as if we'd just been given our ace. "You never know, Winnie."

Pat had Barker, Sal, M, and me meet after school for debate practice, which consisted of her trying to explain the rules. Each of us had to give a one-to-two-minute opening argument. Then we had to know enough to rebut the opposing team's arguments.

Barker promised to compile a list of facts for us to use in the debate since we only had 24 hours to prepare. Sal painted her fingernails during the whole practice. I said three words, and M none. I felt like hurling.

I stopped by the pet shop and answered the Pet Help Line. Hawk's name didn't show in my in-box, and my disappointment surprised me. In school Hawk hung out with the popular kids, and she and I could go a whole day on a couple of hi's. But on e-mail, one day without hearing from her seemed weird.

Just as I finished my last e-mail, advising "Frustrated" to slow down training his horse and focus on one skill at a time, Pat hurried by the computer.

She stopped, then backed up even with me. "How's that hunter coming along?"

"Great, Pat!" I answered, choking on the lie, relieved when she walked away.

Catman followed me home. Our bikes made the cool breeze colder. By the time we reached home, I was glad I'd worn my flannel shirt.

Catman joined Dad at the rocker. I went straight to the pasture to lunge Bold Beauty. Riderless, she sailed over the pole jumps with no problem. I kept telling myself I'd get the debate over with. Then I could really focus on Beauty. I'd be over that high jump with no sweat.

I was leading Beauty back in when I heard a car pull up and two doors slam. Seconds later Richard and Summer walked out to the paddock. Summer still wore the long red sweater she'd worn at school. She looked as out of place as an American Saddle Horse at a Clydesdale convention.

"Can I help you?" I asked, as if they were customers.

"Good! We're in time," Richard announced.

"Time for what?" I led Beauty past them into the barn.

Richard followed me. "Time to watch you jump. I promised the Howards a firsthand report before they come see for themselves."

"Maybe next week, Richard." I hooked Beauty in the cross-ties and starting brushing her.

"Next week?" Richard frowned at his sister, then at me. "Next week's too late. The Howards flew in this morning. They want to see their horse jump tomorrow. Didn't Summer tell you?"

132

Summer shrugged. "Oops! Didn't I tell you the Howards were coming back early, Winnie? Honeymoon hurricanes in the Caribbean. I had Richard tell them to meet us here tomorrow afternoon, since I—*we*—have that debate tomorrow night."

My hands trembled. I slid my arm around Beauty's neck. Trusting, she turned to me, her fate in my hands.

"We really need to see her high jump." Richard sounded impatient. "You're using that hedge out there, right?"

"Right." My voice sounded hoarse.

Catman strolled into the barn and walked up to Beauty. He straightened her forelock. I knew he'd heard everything.

Richard glanced at his watch. "I need to call Jeffrey Howard pretty soon."

I unhooked Beauty from the cross-ties. "Guess I better saddle up then."

Richard and Summer headed back out to the paddock.

Catman helped me saddle Bold Beauty in silence. He handed me the girth under her belly, put the reins over her neck, held her while I mounted.

The mental photo of my fall flashed through my head. *Go away! I'm Winnie the Horse Gentler! I can do this!*

I trotted Beauty in a loose circle around the jumps. Sensing her rhythm, I posted, bobbing up and down in the saddle, moving to a rising trot like Adrianna had. I relaxed as Beauty shifted into a canter, her long legs reaching out, eager to jump.

I guided her to the ground poles that started my jumping course. Stride . . . stride . . . stride . . . jump. No problem. Next came the crossed poles, the low jumps. We sailed over with perfect clearance.

Why had I put this off so long? Beauty and I were born to jump!

I glanced back at Richard and Summer and saw Dad and Lizzy leaning over the fence with Catman.

"The *high* jump, Winnie!" Summer yelled.

Watch this, Summer! I took Beauty around to repeat the course. But this time I rested the reins on her neck, while I stretched my arms out from my sides like airplane wings. Mom had taught me to jump without hands to make sure I'd grip with my legs. Beauty took the low jumps, and I sat tight, my arms still out.

"Yea, Winnie!" Lizzy yelled.

I looped again, making a figure eight, taking the parallel mid-jumps at the diagonal crosses without a flaw.

Lizzy cheered.

"Could you speed it up, Winnie?" Richard shouted.

I knew what he was waiting for. Lizzy might have been impressed, but Richard and Summer knew better. They'd come to see the high jump. Nothing else mattered.

The hedge made up the last jump in the course, rising from the top of my imaginary figure eight. I couldn't put it off any longer.

Beauty sensed what was coming as I started

the course over. We took the low jumps, picked up speed in the middle, and galloped for the hedge.

Throw your heart over the fence, and your horse will follow. I said it over and over in my mind. The hedge grew taller with every stride as we drew closer. Four more strides. Three. Tighten stride.

Or should she lengthen stride? I didn't know. I wasn't sure. And Beauty could feel it. She slowed, then sped up. She'd never make it over.

At the last second, I pulled hard to the left, jerking her away from the hedge. She tossed her head and obeyed, still in a canter, circling away, the hedge behind us now.

I'd refused the jump. Not her. She hadn't balked or stalled. I'd pulled out of the jump. I swallowed the lump in my throat as we trotted up to the barn.

Lizzy balanced herself on the top rung of fence. "That was so tight, Winnie! Aren't you going to jump the hedge?" she asked in pure innocence, as if I'd forgotten one jump by mistake.

Summer let out a harsh laugh. "Yeah, Winnie. Aren't you going to jump the hedge?"

I didn't answer. I kept my head down as I led Beauty past Dad and into the barn.

Richard trailed after me, with Summer at his side. "That's what we needed to see. Thanks, Winnie."

I snapped Beauty into the cross-ties. I couldn't look her in the eyes.

Lizzy, Dad, and Catman walked up. Lizzy still looked puzzled. "Why didn't Winnie jump the hedge?"

Catman whispered something to her, and her expression changed. She shot me a look of pure pity, which hurt worse than anything she could have said.

I glared at Catman, knowing he'd told her I'd chickened out.

"We'll see you in the house, Winnie," Dad said, herding Lizzy and Catman out of the barn.

I kept brushing Beauty, trying not to think about what I'd done. What I'd *not* done. I thought Spidells had left until I heard Richard's voice outside the barn.

"Glad I caught you! I'm at the Willis place." He was talking on the cell phone. "No, Winnie hasn't had any more luck with this horse than we did." He chuckled. "She's a good kid all right.

And very talented too, when it comes to ordinary horses. . . . Wait 'til you see the hunter I've found for you. More money, but can he jump!"

He paused. My ears buzzed. I couldn't breathe.

Richard chuckled. "Your wife will come around. Tell her not to worry about the mare. I've made some calls to a camp in Columbus. . . . I agree. Poor Winnie did her best, but she couldn't handle the high jump. . . . Sure! Tomorrow afternoon, right here. I'll bring the trailer. Glad I could help."

Summer honked, and I listened to the gravel crunch as Richard ran to his car.

I hung out in the barn, saddle-soaping tack, scrubbing the soft soap into saddles and bridles until they foamed clean and shiny. Anything so I didn't have to talk to humans.

It was dark when Lizzy came looking for me. "You okay?"

"I'm fine!" I insisted, pushing past her and outside, where stars winked at each other.

"It's okay to lose your confidence, Winnie. Everybody—"

I wheeled on her. "Who said I lost my confidence? Catman? Well, I didn't!" I stormed toward the house. Lucky for Catman, I didn't see him anywhere.

Lizzy dogged me. "You should have told Dad and me!"

"There's nothing to tell!" I screamed, making it to the front steps.

"Winnie?" Dad shouted from the shed.

I pretended not to hear.

I ran to the bedroom, slammed the door, kicked off my boots, slipped into my pj's, and dove into bed. I hadn't lost my confidence! That was ridiculous.

A long time later I heard Lizzy come in. I pretended to be asleep as she got ready for bed and clicked on her reading light.

A knock came at the door.

"Come on in, Dad!" Lizzy called.

I didn't budge. The door opened, and footsteps crossed to my bed. I squeezed my eyes shut. The footsteps moved to Lizzy's side of the room.

"Night, Lizzy," Dad whispered.

"Night, Dad." Then Lizzy slipped into praying: "God, thanks for being Immanuel. Help Winnie turn around and see that you're in that boat with her."

I knew she was talking about what Ralph had said in church, about Peter and the other fishermen and the storm, and Jesus sleeping in the boat. But I didn't care. All that mattered was Bold Beauty. I'd let her down. And tomorrow she'd be gone forever.

Dad left, and Lizzy read for a few minutes before turning off the light. Within seconds I heard the Lizzy-snore I'd known my whole life.

I sat up in bed. The full moon shined a spotlight through the window. White streams of light washed the pasture. I could see the outline of the hedge. In a few hours Bold Beauty would be taken away to a place where no one would think of her as a hunter. She'd be condemned to ride in circles, tugged on by riders who didn't love her like I did or like Adrianna would.

Unless . . .

I stared out at the hedge moving in the wind like a living thing. *Why can't you psych yourself into this, Winnie?*

Maybe I'd pulled Beauty up because Summer and Richard made me nervous. If I could jump when nobody was around . . .

Why not? There was absolutely no reason Beauty and I couldn't clear that jump. And if I could get her over the hedge one time, then I could show Adrianna. It wouldn't be too late!

I could do it! I had to.

Chapter 13

I pulled jeans over my pj's and boots over my bare feet and slipped outside. Dew drenched the fallen leaves and lurked in the cold, damp air. I moved through the barn as if in a dream, saddling and bridling Bold Beauty while Nickers and Towaco looked on.

Before I could stop myself, I mounted Beauty and guided her to the jumps. I knew every inch of the pasture. The ground shimmered in painted moonlight. I could do this. Of course I could.

Beauty and I cantered. An owl hooted. Crickets chirped louder and louder, in waves. We took the low jumps, the middle jumps. She picked up her pace as we galloped for the hedge. Faster and faster. No turning back. "We can do this, Beauty!"

But it was a lie. I could lie to my family. I could lie to myself. But I couldn't lie to Bold Beauty. Doubts and fear traveled through my skin to my fingers, through the reins, to the bit, where Beauty swallowed them. She hesitated.

Throw your heart over!

But hers wouldn't go, and neither would mine. Our hearts were wound together liked trapped insects in a spider's web.

She stopped short in front of the hedge. I slid off, landing on my feet, and then collapsed to the ground, not sure if I'd fallen or given up.

"Winnie!" Catman came running up. "Man, I told Claire and Bart you'd freak out tonight! They gave me the go-ahead to spy. I knew you'd try something like this no matter how scared you were!"

I opened my mouth to deny being scared. But the lies had drained out of me, leaving me with nothing. I buried my head in my hands. Tears flowed with noisy sobs that wracked my whole body.

When I could get my breath again, I gazed up

at Catman. "What's wrong with me? I'm afraid of that stupid hedge!"

Catman took off his glasses and shoved them into his pocket. "Finally."

"Finally what?" I yelled.

"Finally you can admit it. That's cool."

The fake confidence I'd tried to hold on to slipped away. Something would have to replace it. But for now, it was enough to break out of the web with the truth. I'd been afraid to jump that hedge.

Catman took off Beauty's saddle and bridle. Beauty went back to grazing with Towaco and Nickers, and Catman walked me to the door.

"Thanks, Catman." It didn't seem like much to say.

He held up thumb and pinkie in the Hawaiian hang-loose sign and disappeared into the night.

I crawled into bed and talked to God. *Sorry about the stupid lies, God. You don't deserve that. Please forgive me. I'm done with lies and fake confidence. I'm out of ideas on how to save Beauty or get*

over that hedge by tomorrow. But I know you're in the boat with me. So thanks.

I felt a hundred times better as I crawled under the quilt, even though I knew there was still a piece missing, something I wasn't getting. No way did I want to psyche up a false confidence again. But if I wanted to save Beauty, wouldn't I need some kind of confidence? I tried to figure it out as sleep pressed against my eyeballs.

I'd almost drifted into sleep when I remembered the debate. *And God, would you cover for me in that debate, too? Amen.*

Saturday morning I woke up from the best night's sleep I'd had in days. I had no idea how things would turn out—with the Howards or the debate. But I knew I wasn't in it alone.

I couldn't wait to tell Lizzy how sorry I was for shutting her out and lying to her about everything. But she'd already left on a lizard hunt. I showered, dressed, and ran outside to find Dad.

He was speed-rocking in his latest invention, but the little fan at the top barely turned.

"Dad!" I shouted.

The rocking slowed, then stopped. Sweat trickled down his neck.

"Dad, I'm sorry about last night. And the other nights. I should have told you about the hedge. I just didn't want to admit I lost my confidence."

"I know." He looked straight into my eyes, and I could almost feel his forgiveness.

"Last night I—"

But Dad interrupted. "Isn't this rocker-powered chair a hoot, Winnie?"

"What?" Even now, Dad couldn't stop talking about his inventions?

"I've been rocking with all my power, not even getting a tiny wind to help cool me off." He leaned back in the chair, his legs crossed at the ankles. "Now will you look at this?" He closed his eyes. "God sends me a perfect breeze without even trying."

"Dad, will you listen a—?" I shut my mouth. *God sends the breeze without even trying?*

"That's it! Dad, you're a genius!" My dad had just given me the missing piece to my confidence puzzle. And I was sure he had no idea that I needed it! Maybe *I* couldn't lick that hedge, but God could!

Weird that admitting I couldn't jump that

hedge without God's help should make me feel more self-confident than I'd ever felt in my whole life, but it did.

I kissed Dad's forehead and took off for Pat's Pets on the back bike. I let myself in with the key Pat leaves in the flowerpot in case we have to man the help line after hours. I wanted to e-mail Hawk before she got home from Paris. They were flying in today. She'd been honest with me about being afraid to talk to her parents, and all I'd done was try to give her fake confidence.

As I waited for the computer to boot, I prayed that Hawk would check her e-mail on the plane. Then I typed:

> Hawk!
> URGENT! Truth is, I haven't been doing well with Bold Beauty. I fell off trying to get her over the high-jump hedge. Until last night, I'd faked it, pretending I still had my old confidence. But I don't, Hawk. So don't feel so bad about being scared to talk to your parents.

I tried to think how to say the rest. Hawk and I had never talked about God. She didn't go to church. Our friendship was fragile enough without having her think I'd turned into a Jesus freak on her. On the other hand, how could I stop being honest now?

I finished my note:

> I don't know what you think about God and Jesus, Hawk. And I don't know as much about God as Lizzy and Pat and Barker do. But I do know that's where I'm going to get my confidence. My mom used to say that when we come to the end of ourselves, we come to the beginning of God. That's where I am with Beauty, Hawk. Hope you're reading this.
> —Winnie

"I reckon that's about the best answer I've ever read on the help line."

I twirled around to see Pat Haven, still dressed in a flannel nightgown, her hair looking like she'd just survived an electrical shock.

"Pat! I'm sorry about everything. I should have told you. I fell off Bold Beauty. I haven't gotten her over that hedge even once."

"Well, duh. You think I'm dumber than a duck,

no offense? Love those little creatures. I figured you'd tell me when you got around to it."

I stood up and hugged her. "Pat, pray for me. The Howards are coming for Bold Beauty. I want the chance to face that hedge knowing what I know now."

"Then scoot!" Pat nearly shoved me out the door. "And don't forget our debate tonight!"

When I biked into our yard, Lizzy was standing with Dad, while Catman was taking his turn in the rocker. She handed me her can of pop.

"Thanks, Lizzy." I took a big drink. "And I'm sorry for not—"

She cut me off with a shake of her head. "It's okay. Catman filled us in. But Richard called, Winnie. They're on their way here. Are you going to be okay?"

Catman stopped rocking. He and Dad stared at me.

"You bet! Bold Beauty and I have a hedge to jump."

Saying it didn't make me feel like hurling this time. All week long I'd lied to myself, thinking that was how I'd get the confidence I needed. But this was different. I knew I wasn't in the boat alone.

They didn't say anything.

"Don't worry," I said. "That hedge might be too big for me. But God made the hedge, right? How could it be too big for him?"

Before Dad could object, I dashed inside to change. As I sat on the bed and pulled on boots, something crunched inside my left boot. I reached inside and pulled out an index card. On it was printed:

> *In your strength I can crush an army; with my God I can scale any wall. He makes me as surefooted as a deer, leading me safely along the mountain heights.*
>
> —2 Samuel 22:30, 34

With my God I can scale any wall. Leave it to Lizzy to come up with the perfect verse. I stuck it in my pocket and ran out to the barn.

I'd just finished saddling Beauty when I heard Spidells' trailer drive up and a car just after it. Doors slammed as Summer and Richard climbed down from the trailer and the Howards got out of their car. Lizzy's voice floated across the yard as she stalled them.

By the time they made it to the barn, I'd led Beauty all around the hedge, letting her sniff and study it while I stroked her and promised everything would be all right.

I swung myself up into the saddle as the Howards walked over. When I waved to Adrianna, she waved back. I knew she'd be rooting for Beauty.

Richard's smile faded as he turned to me. "Winnie, ride the mare over here! We need to load her."

"Not quite yet!" I shouted, cantering by them. My heart was galloping, but not from fear . . . from excitement.

Only a few hours had passed since I'd tried the hedge, but nothing felt the same. This time I was riding double. God was there in the rhythm of the hoofbeats, the breath of Bold Beauty.

We cantered the loops, taking the cross jumps with no effort. I felt Beauty gather her muscles, anticipating the big jump. We looked at it straight on. But neither of us tensed or stiffened.

Beauty had her lead as she stretched into a gallop and aimed for the hedge. As if we were in a ballet, I heard nothing but the muffled hooves in dirt, the horse music pounding strong and confident.

I saw the hedge framed between her ears, and it rose green and full of life, not too tall, not for us. *With my God I can scale any wall!* We closed in on the hedge. *Thu-dump, thu-dump, thu-dump.* And there it was.

My heart sailed over, and so did Bold Beauty's. Then we followed, soaring, as if flying heaven-bound, carried by God.

Beauty landed on the other side without so much as scuffing a hoof on the hedge. She kept cantering, looking for more. I gave her more. We circled back and took the hedge again. And again.

Finally, I turned her back toward the paddock, reaching down to stroke her neck. "Good girl, Beauty!" I whispered.

"That was marvelous!" Adrianna shouted, rushing out to us and throwing her arms around her horse's neck.

Lizzy cheered. Dad clapped. Catman snapped his fingers.

Red-faced, Summer looked like she might cry.

"That's still a temperamental horse," Richard insisted. "Just because she got over the hedge a few times—"

"Beauty could do it a million times," I said quietly. "Would you like us to go again?"

"That won't be necessary." Adrianna looked from her horse to me. Something passed between us, like two horses reading each other without words, like horse lovers sharing something nobody else could understand. For a second I felt sorry for Summer and Richard. They'd never have what we have with horses. They'd never feel what we feel.

"Winnie," Adrianna said, "you have a gift."

"And you have a gifted horse," I replied.

"I have to go home," Summer muttered. When her brother didn't respond, she raised her voice. "Richard, I said I want to go home!"

Mr. Howard shook Richard's hand. They talked a minute. Then Richard and Summer left in their empty trailer.

The Howards congratulated me again, then drove off with the promise to return for their horse after I'd worked with her for another week—long enough to give Beauty *real* confidence.

Catman walked up and straightened Beauty's forelock. "Groovy." Then he turned and walked away.

"Thanks, Catman! For everything!" I hollered after him.

He made the peace sign and kept on walking.

I turned to Lizzy and Dad.

"You did it!" Lizzy cried, throwing her arms around me.

I hugged her back. "Thanks, Lizzy. And thanks for the verses."

Lizzy stepped back. "What verses?"

"In my boot? Especially the one about scaling any wall. It went over and over in my head when we jumped."

Lizzy frowned. "I didn't give you any verses."

"But you—" I stopped and turned to my dad. "Dad?"

He shrugged. "I found it when I was hunting up some confidence for myself. Thought you might like it."

I walked over and hugged him awkwardly. He fiddled with the keys in his pocket and looked away.

A picture flashed into my mind—Dad sitting back in his rocker, talking about God's breeze. And he'd put that verse in my boot? Something told me I had a lot to learn about my dad.

Dad broke the silence between us. "Am I

wrong, or do you have a debate to go to today?"

The debate! I may have just jumped a huge hurdle. But an even bigger one was still out there.

It took Lizzy so long to wrestle my tangled hair into a French braid that I was the last debater to show up at middle school. I took my seat at our team's table, between Sal, dressed in a neon green shirt that matched the streak in her hair, and M, wearing his all-black uniform. A few feet over, Ms. Brumby and her team—Summer, Kristine, Brian, and Grant—looked relaxed, laughing as if they had the debate already sewn up.

"They go first with opening statements," Pat explained. "After their team captain gives his statement, Barker gives his. Then we'll go back and forth until all statements are presented. After that, Ms. Brumby opens the floor for rebuttals. Remember, don't let 'em get your goat—no offense!"

My stomach tried to push up everything in it. I glanced out at the gym floor. Chairs were filling fast. The Barkers, with Dad and Lizzy and Catman, took up the whole front row.

Then in strolled Hawk with Peter Lory on her shoulder. She'd made it! Hawk waved at Summer and squinted toward us. When she saw me, she shouted, "Good e-mail! I told them!"

Thanks, God, I prayed, again feeling him in the boat with me.

"Here, Winnie!" Barker handed me an information sheet on the development of an unborn baby. "You can read from it for your opening statement."

"Time to turn in notes!" Ms. Brumby stood over me, her hand out.

I gripped the page with both hands.

Ms. Brumby turned to me. "Don't you know that notes are not allowed? It's in the manual."

"Well, I was thinking . . . since we haven't had much time to practice. . . ," Pat began. Then she took the sheet from me. "But you're right. Rules are rules. We'll do just fine without it."

Right. If I couldn't read it, I'd never say anything that made sense!

Note to self: Switch sides so you can ruin Summer's team instead.

Ms. Brumby welcomed everyone. Then Grant launched into his opening statement about abortion being legal and women needing rights over their own bodies.

But Barker defined abortion as destroying the life of a developing child. He didn't say it like he was accusing anybody, but like he was your best friend helping you understand something important. He finished by squarely facing the other team. "From the moment that baby is created, he or she has everything needed to be an individual—with DNA unlike anybody ever born! God made each person unique."

"He said *God* in the school gym, Ms. Brumby!" Summer cried, standing up. "Can he do that?"

Grant pulled Summer down by her sleeve.

Kristine looked nervous as she gave her statement, but her voice didn't shake. "This is a hard question," she admitted. "But I keep thinking about women who just can't do a good job raising a child. What about someone who's been raped? Should she have to raise that baby? Wouldn't the child have a sad life? That's why I think the mother should choose."

It was the best argument so far from their side. I knew Barker would have something to say in rebuttal about how few pregnancies resulted from rape and about doing what was right no matter what. But you had to hand it to Kristine. I didn't know her at all, except as Summer's sidekick. But she sounded sincere, like she'd wrestled with stuff.

Sal came next. I had no idea what she'd say.

"I'm definitely for choice!" Sal announced.

"Sal!" I whispered. "You can't change sides now!"

Sal continued as if she hadn't heard me. "That unborn baby should get to choose. Poor little kid can't make you hear him. But you know what he'd choose, right? Life! Who wouldn't?"

"Way to go, Sal!" I whispered. I hardly heard Brian's statement, knowing I was up next.

"Winnie?" Ms. Brumby turned to me.

"I . . ." There were so many things I should say, but my throat closed and my tongue had turned to velcro.

Summer snickered.

I stared out into the gym. Lizzy's eyes were as big as a draft horse's. But Dad just grinned, like he wasn't worried one bit.

And then I remembered: *With my God I can scale any wall.* In that instant, my mind flashed me a perfect photo image of Barker's fact sheet. I could read it word for word. I opened my mouth and prayed that God would kick the words out. "Abortions usually aren't done before seven weeks." My voice sounded hoarse but loud enough. "By then, the baby's heart has been beating for almost four weeks. She has her own blood, maybe a different type from her mom's. He's got arms and legs you could pick out in a photo, eyes and hands, brain waves. Sometimes you can make out fingers, eyelids, toes, a nose."

I thought of something from a news report Dad and I had seen when we lived in one of the *I* states. I looked over and smiled at Kristine. She smiled back. "If Kristine were pregnant and I shot her, I could be found guilty of two murders—hers and her unborn baby's."

"No fooling?" Sal asked.

"Some of you remember when your little brothers or sisters were born," I continued, not reading the sheet any longer, trusting God and myself.

Kids mumbled from the gym. Even Summer

seemed to be listening. Kristine said she remembered.

"Your folks named the baby, felt kicks, and waited. All of you knew—that was a person in there."

Summer interrupted. "Time's up! My turn. We're too young to remember what people called 'back-alley abortions,' the dangerous things women had to do to their bodies before abortions were legal." She gave her statement, filled with statistics and facts, without a single *uh* or *um*. She finished strong on abortion as a woman's right. "I'm a woman. And if I were pregnant, *I'd* be the one who'd have to take care of the child. So, if I wanted an abortion, I'd have one."

I felt sorry for M when Ms. Brumby told him to give his statement. He mumbled, "Don't do it."

Ms. Brumby tried to cover for him and moved on to open rebuttals. "Would anyone like to address an opponent's argument at this point?"

So far in the debate, M had stared down at our table, showing no emotion, no sign he'd even heard the arguments. So when he turned to Summer and uttered one word, it had the force of a shout. "When?"

"When what?" Summer asked.

"When would you have your abortion?" M asked, his voice clear.

"Whenever I please!" Summer leaned back and crossed her arms in front of her.

"A year old?" M asked, his voice firm. "Kid's a lot of work then."

"Of course not!" Summer said it like M stood for Moron.

"A second before birth?" M asked.

"No! Before that!" Summer snapped.

"On the way to the hospital?"

"Before then." But Summer's answers were losing force.

"A month before?" M pressed.

"Earlier."

M kept at it, forcing Summer to back down—not seven months, not six, not five. Two babies right here in Ohio were born when they were four and a half and five months old. And they were normal, M told us.

"You can't pick a time because life starts at conception," M stated. "No other point where you can draw a life line."

Finally Summer lost it. "Nobody tells me I can't make my own choice!"

"Choose adoption," M said simply. "That's what my bio mom did. And my folks and I are glad she did."

Two people dressed totally in black stood up and cheered. "Go, M!"

Grant laughed out loud. "Can't argue with that."

Ms. Brumby ended the debate. "Thanks to both teams for a thought-provoking debate. Mrs. Haven and I will be tallying scores and awarding points. But I'd say you all did an admirable job. Congratulations." She clapped and everyone else followed her lead.

Grant hollered over, "M, you're really something!"

Summer wheeled on him. "I don't know why anybody would listen to a creep who wears black every day of his life!"

"Summer!" I shouted. "Better check those facts! M is only wearing black until they come up with a darker color."

Catman hopped up onstage, snapping his fingers, his hippie/beatnik way of clapping. M gave me a high five. Barker thanked all of us, while Pat hugged everybody on both teams.

I made my way down to Lizzy and Dad. Lizzy

hugged me and said all the right things before a bunch of her classmates came and swept her away. She was spending the night at her friend Katy's house.

Dad and I walked out together in time to see Barker's family pile into their yellow bus.

The cattle truck started on the fourth try. "Great job, Winnie!" Dad said, backing out and turning toward home. "I wish I had your confidence."

"You? You're not afraid of anything." I grinned over at him. "Except riding horses."

"You knew?" he asked.

"Yeah, Dad."

"I've ridden a couple of times—for your mother. She laughed so hard. . . ."

We were quiet for a minute, but it was a good quiet.

He turned onto our street, and the moon shone directly ahead of us. "Lately though, I've been more afraid of that contest Catman has been after me to enter."

"That's why you kept putting off filling out that entry form?" The thought of my dad not having confidence in his inventions had never entered my mind.

"Guess I was afraid of losing, of having to admit I'm not an inventor, just an out-of-work insurance salesman."

I started to tell him that was crazy, but he held up his hand for me to stop. "Anyway, after you jumped that hedge, I went in the house and filled out that contest entry form—on the back bike, not the rocker." He pulled a rolled-up paper from his coat pocket. "The deadline is midnight tonight. Now all I have to do is have the guts to mail it."

He pulled up in front of our house. The cab of the truck felt as full as the Barker van on Sunday morning, crowded with memories of my mom, and overflowing with *Immanuel,* God with us.

"Dad!" I cried. "I've got an idea."

Chapter 15

*M*inutes later Nickers strolled out of the barn with my dad and me riding double. Dad sat stiffly behind me, holding on so tight it was hard for me to breathe. In one hand he clutched the contest entry.

Nickers whinnied as she *clip-clopp*ed down our street. The wind howled at our backs the three blocks to the mailbox. I guided my mare close to the mail slot and pulled down the handle.

Dad hesitated.

"With my God, I can scale a wall!" I declared.

Dad sighed and shoved in the contest entry. "With my God, I can enter a contest!"

Nickers turned and headed home under a blanket of stars, windblown leaves showering us.

"With my God, I can speak in a debate!" I shouted.

"And ride a horse!" Dad yelled.

"And stand up to Summer!"

"And . . ."

We laughed at each other. But it felt true, as if we could go on and on, riding against the wind, the sound of Nickers' hooves steady and sure, and the possibilities endless.

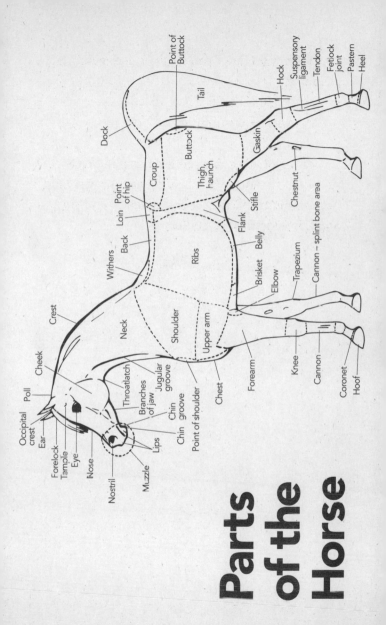

Parts
of the
Horse

🐎 Horse Talk!

Horses communicate with one another . . . and with us, if we learn to read their cues. Here are some of the main ways a horse talks:

Whinny—A loud, long horse call that can be heard from a half mile away. Horses often whinny back and forth.
Possible translations: *Is that you over there? Hello! I'm over here! See me? I heard you! What's going on?*

Neigh—To most horse people, a neigh is the same as a whinny. Some people call any vocalization from a horse a neigh.

Nicker—The friendliest horse greeting in the world. A nicker is a low sound made in the throat, sometimes rumbling. Horses use it as a warm greeting for another horse or a trusted person. A horse owner might hear a nicker at feeding time.
Possible translations: *Welcome back! Good to see you. I missed you. Hey there! Come on over. Got anything good to eat?*

Snort—This sounds like your snort, only much louder and more fluttering. It's a hard exhale, with the air being forced out through the nostrils.
Possible translations: *Look out! Something's wrong out there! Yikes! What's that?*

Blow—Usually one huge exhale, like a snort, but in a large burst of wind.
Possible translations: *What's going on? Things aren't so bad. Such is life.*

Squeal—This high-pitched cry that sounds a bit like a scream can be heard a hundred yards away.
Possible translations: *Don't you dare! Stop it! I'm warning you! I've had it—I mean it! That hurts!*

Grunts, groans, sighs, sniffs—Horses make a variety of sounds. Some grunts and groans mean nothing more than boredom. Others are natural outgrowths of exercise.

★★★★★

Horses also communicate without making a sound. You'll need to observe each horse and tune in to the individual translations, but here are some possible versions of nonverbal horse talk:

EARS
Flat back ears—When a horse pins back its ears, pay attention and beware! If the ears go back slightly, the

horse may just be irritated. The closer the ears are pressed back to the skull, the angrier the horse.

Possible translations: *I don't like that buzzing fly. You're making me mad! I'm warning you! You try that, and I'll make you wish you hadn't!*

Pricked forward, stiff ears—Ears stiffly forward usually mean a horse is on the alert. Something ahead has captured its attention.

Possible translations: *What's that? Did you hear that? I want to know what that is! Forward ears may also say, I'm cool and proud of it!*

Relaxed, loosely forward ears—When a horse is content, listening to sounds all around, ears relax, tilting loosely forward.

Possible translations: *It's a fine day, not too bad at all. Nothin' new out here.*

Uneven ears—When a horse swivels one ear up and one ear back, it's just paying attention to the surroundings.

Possible translations: *Sigh. So, anything interesting going on yet?*

Stiff, twitching ears—If a horse twitches stiff ears, flicking them fast (in combination with overall body tension), be on guard! This horse may be terrified and ready to bolt.

Possible translations: *Yikes! I'm outta here! Run for the hills!*

Airplane ears—Ears lopped to the sides usually means the horse is bored or tired.

Possible translations: *Nothing ever happens around here. So, what's next already? Bor-ing.*

Droopy ears—When a horse's ears sag and droop to the sides, it may just be sleepy, or it might be in pain.

Possible translations: *Yawn . . . I am so sleepy. I could sure use some shut-eye. I don't feel so good. It really hurts.*

TAIL

Tail switches hard and fast—An intensely angry horse will switch its tail hard enough to hurt anyone foolhardy enough to stand within striking distance. The tail flies side to side and maybe up and down as well.

Possible translations: *I've had it, I tell you! Enough is enough! Stand back and get out of my way!*

Tail held high—A horse who holds its tail high may be proud to be a horse!

Possible translations: *Get a load of me! Hey! Look how gorgeous I am! I'm so amazing that I just may hightail it out of here!*

Clamped-down tail—Fear can make a horse clamp its tail to its rump.

Possible translations: *I don't like this; it's scary. What are they going to do to me? Can't somebody help me?*

Pointed tail swat—One sharp, well-aimed swat of the tail could mean something hurts there.
Possible translations: Ouch! That hurts! Got that pesky fly.

OTHER SIGNALS

Pay attention to other body language. Stamping a hoof may mean impatience or eagerness to get going. A rear hoof raised slightly off the ground might be a sign of irritation. The same hoof raised, but relaxed, may signal sleepiness. When a horse is angry, the muscles tense, back stiffens, and the eyes flash, showing extra white of the eyeballs. One anxious horse may balk, standing stone still and stiff legged. Another horse just as anxious may dance sideways or paw the ground. A horse in pain might swing its head backward toward the pain, toss its head, shiver, or try to rub or nibble the sore spot. Sick horses tend to lower their heads and look dull, listless, and unresponsive.

As you attempt to communicate with your horse and understand what he or she is saying, remember that different horses may use the same sound or signal, but mean different things. One horse may flatten her ears in anger, while another horse lays back his ears to listen to a rider. Each horse has his or her own language, and it's up to you to understand.

🐎 Horse-O-Pedia

American Saddlebred (or American Saddle Horse)—A showy breed of horse with five gaits (walk, trot, canter, and two extras). They are usually high-spirited, often high-strung; mainly seen in horse shows.

Andalusian—A breed of horse originating in Spain, strong and striking in appearance. They have been used in dressage, as parade horses, in the bullring, and even for herding cattle.

Appaloosa—Horse with mottled skin and a pattern of spots, such as a solid white or brown with oblong, dark spots behind the withers. They're usually good all-around horses.

Arabian—Believed to be the oldest breed or one of the oldest. Arabians are thought by many to be the most beautiful of all horses. They are characterized by a small head, large eyes, refined build, silky mane and tail, and often high spirits.

Barb—North African desert horse.

Bay—A horse with a mahogany or deep brown to reddish-brown color and a black mane and tail.

Blind-age—Without revealing age.

Buck—To thrust out the back legs, kicking off the ground.

Buckskin—Tan or grayish-yellow-colored horse with black mane and tail.

Canter—A rolling gait with a three-time pace slower than a gallop. The rhythm falls with the right hind foot, then the left hind and right fore simultaneously, then the left fore followed by a period of suspension when all feet are off the ground.

Cattle-pony stop—Sudden, sliding stop with drastically bent haunches and rear legs; the type of stop a cutting, or cowboy, horse might make to round up cattle.

Chestnut—A horse with a coat colored golden yellow to dark brown, sometimes the color of bays, but with same-color mane and tail.

Cloverleaf—The three-cornered racing pattern followed in many barrel races; so named because the circles around each barrel resemble the three petals on a clover leaf.

Conformation—The overall structure of a horse; the way his parts fit together. Good conformation in a horse means that horse is solidly built, with straight legs and well-proportioned features.

Crop—A small whip sometimes used by riders.

Cross-ties—Two straps coming from opposite walls of the stallway. They hook onto a horse's halter for easier grooming.

Curb—A single-bar bit with a curve in the middle and shanks and a curb chain to provide leverage in a horse's mouth.

D ring—The D-shaped, metal ring on the side of a horse's halter.

English Riding—The style of riding English or Eastern or Saddle Seat, on a flat saddle that's lighter and leaner than a Western saddle. English riding is seen in three-gaited and five-gaited Saddle Horse classes in horse shows. In competition, the rider posts at the trot and wears a formal riding habit.

Gait—Set manner in which a horse moves. Horses have four natural gaits: the walk, the trot or jog, the canter or lope, and the gallop. Other gaits have been learned or are characteristic to certain breeds: pace, amble, slow gait, rack, running walk, etc.

Gelding—An altered male horse.

Hackamore—A bridle with no bit, often used for training Western horses.

Halter—Basic device of straps or rope fitting around a horse's head and behind the ears. Halters are used to lead or tie up a horse.

Hunter—A horse used primarily for hunt riding. Hunter is a type, not a distinct breed. Many hunters are bred in Ireland, Britain, and the U.S.

Leadrope—A rope with a hook on one end to attach to a horse's halter for leading or tying the horse.

Leads—The act of a horse galloping in such a way as to balance his body, leading with one side or the other. In a *right lead*, the right foreleg leaves the ground last and seems to reach out farther. In a *left lead*, the horse reaches out farther with the left foreleg, usually when galloping counterclockwise.

Lipizzaner—Strong, stately horse used in the famous Spanish Riding School of Vienna. Lipizzaners are born black and turn gray or white.

Lunge line (longe line)—A very long lead line or rope, used for exercising a horse from the ground. A hook at one end of the line is attached to the horse's halter, and the horse is encouraged to move in a circle around the handler.

Lusitano—Large, agile, noble breed of horse from Portugal. They're known as the mounts of bullfighters.

Mare—Female horse.

Morgan—A compact, solidly built breed of horse with muscular shoulders. Morgans are usually reliable, trustworthy horses.

Mustang—Originally, a small, hardy Spanish horse turned loose in the wilds. Mustangs still run wild in protected parts of the U.S. They are suspicious of humans, tough, hard to train, but quick and able horses.

Paddock—Fenced area near a stable or barn; smaller than a pasture. It's often used for training and working horses.

Paint—A spotted horse with Quarter Horse or Thoroughbred bloodlines. The American Paint Horse Association registers only those horses with Paint, Quarter Horse, or Thoroughbred registration papers.

Palomino—Cream-colored or golden horse with a silver or white mane and tail.

Palouse—Native American people who inhabited the Washington–Oregon area. They were highly skilled in horse training and are credited with developing the Appaloosas.

Pinto—Spotted horse, brown and white or black and white. Refers only to color. The Pinto Horse Association registers any spotted horse or pony.

Post—A riding technique in English horsemanship. The rider posts to a rising trot, lifting slightly out of the saddle and back down, in coordination with the horse's bounciest gait, the trot.

Przewalski—Perhaps the oldest breed of primitive horse. Also known as the Mongolian Wild Horse, the Przewalski Horse looks primitive, with a large head and a short, broad body.

Quarter Horse—A muscular "cowboy" horse reminiscent of the Old West. The Quarter Horse got its name from the fact that it can outrun other horses over the quarter mile. Quarter Horses are usually easygoing and good-natured.

Quirt—A short-handled rawhide whip sometimes used by riders.

Rear—To suddenly lift both front legs into the air and stand only on the back legs.

Roan—The color of a horse when white hairs mix with the basic coat of black, brown, chestnut, or gray.

Snaffle—A single bar bit, often jointed, or "broken" in

the middle, with no shank. Snaffle bits are generally considered less punishing than curbed bits.

Sorrel—Used to describe a horse that's reddish (usually reddish-brown) in color.

Spur—A short metal spike or spiked wheel that straps to the heel of a rider's boots. Spurs are used to urge the horse on faster.

Stallion—An unaltered male horse.

Standardbred—A breed of horse heavier than the Thoroughbred, but similar in type. Standardbreds have a calm temperament and are used in harness racing.

Tack—Horse equipment (saddles, bridles, halters, etc.).

Tennessee Walker—A gaited horse, with a running walk—half walk and half trot. Tennessee Walking Horses are generally steady and reliable, very comfortable to ride.

Thoroughbred—The fastest breed of horse in the world, they are used as racing horses. Thoroughbreds are often high-strung.

Tie short—Tying the rope with little or no slack to prevent movement from the horse.

Trakehner—Strong, dependable, agile horse that can do it all—show, dressage, jump, harness.

Twitch—A device some horsemen use to make a horse go where it doesn't want to go. A rope noose loops around the upper lip. The loop is attached to what looks like a bat, and the bat is twisted, tightening the noose around the horse's muzzle until he gives in.

Western Riding—The style of riding as cowboys of the Old West rode, as ranchers have ridden, with a traditional Western saddle, heavy, deep-seated, with a raised saddle horn. Trail riding and pleasure riding are generally Western; more relaxed than English riding.

Wind sucking—The bad, and often dangerous, habit of some stabled horses to chew on fence or stall wood and suck in air.

🐎 Author Talk

Dandi Daley Mackall grew up riding horses, taking her first solo bareback ride when she was three. Her best friends were Sugar, a Pinto; Misty, probably a Morgan; and Towaco, an Appaloosa; along with Ash Bill, a Quarter Horse; Rocket, a buckskin; Angel, the colt; Butch, anybody's guess; Lancer and Cindy, American Saddlebreds; and Moby, a white Quarter Horse. Dandi and husband, Joe; daughters, Jen and Katy; and son, Dan (when forced) enjoy riding Cheyenne, their Paint. Dandi has written books for all ages, including Little Blessings books, Degrees of Guilt: *Kyra's Story,* Degrees of Betrayal: *Sierra's Story, Love Rules,* and *Maggie's Story.* Her books (about 400 titles) have sold more than 4 million copies. She writes and rides from rural Ohio.

Visit Dandi at www.dandibooks.com

Winnie
The Horse Gentler

 1 WILD THING

 2 EAGER STAR

 3 BOLD BEAUTY

 4 MIDNIGHT MYSTERY

 5 UNHAPPY APPY

 6 GIFT HORSE

 7 FRIENDLY FOAL

8 BUCKSKIN BANDIT

COLLECT ALL EIGHT BOOKS!

CP0015-B

Can't get enough of Winnie? Visit her Web site to read more about
Winnie and her friends plus all about their horses.

IT'S ALL ON WINNIETHEHORSEGENTLER.COM
There are so many fun and cool things to do on Winnie's Web site; here
are just a few:

★ PAT'S PETS
Post your favorite photo of your pet and tell us a fun story about them

★ ASK WINNIE
Here's your chance to ask Winnie questions about your horse

★ MANE ATTRACTION
Meet Dandi and her horse, Chestnut!

★ THE BARNYARD
Here's your chance to share your
thoughts with others

★ AND MUCH MORE!